Mind to Mind

Mind to Mind

Nine Stories of Science Fiction

Edited by
ROBERT SILVERBERG

WILDSIDE PRESS

www.wildsidebooks.com

ACKNOWLEDGMENTS

"The Mindworm," by C. M. Kornbluth, copyright 1950 by Hillman Periodicals, Inc. Reprinted by permission of Robert P. Mills, Ltd., agent for the author's estate.

Contents

Mind to Mind

Introduction

Problems of communication lie at the core of most human difficulties. Parents and children, husbands and wives, employers and employees, eastern nations and western ones, Arabs and Israelis, Marxists and capitalists—if only they spoke the same language, if only they could each understand what the other was really driving at, how much less strife there would be in the world! But human beings must communicate by means of words, and words are a notoriously inexact medium for conveying information. The same word may have a host of different meanings and shades of meaning. It may be interpreted differently by different people. A country that calls itself a "People's Democratic Republic" may actually be a repressive dictatorship; a politician advocating "law and order" may really be calling for injustice and oppression. No one has yet invented a better method for the exchange of ideas than the use of words, but no one can deny that verbal communication leaves a great deal to be desired.

Science fiction, which of course is greatly concerned with problems of communication, has its own answer to the question of a substitute for the use of words: telepathy, the direct linking of one mind with another. "Telepathy," a word invented about a hundred years ago, is derived from the Greek words for "far off" and "feeling"; but the idea of telepathy is much older than the word itself, since to have the power of looking into the minds of others is one of mankind's most ancient dreams. Actually, science-fiction writers rarely speak of telepathy any more, for newer words have been coined to describe the same phenomena: ESP, for example, short for extra sensory perception, and *psi*, a catch-all term for all the extrasensory powers, and *psionics*, the wishful name for the science of psi that may someday evolve. Under whatever name, though, the science-fiction writer is interested in examining the potentialities of mind-to-mind contact. How can it be achieved? By some sort of amplification of the brain's electrical impulses? By a radical mutation of the human nervous system? By the use of drugs? If we did have telepathy, how would one guard one's privacy? Would one *want* to guard one's privacy? What possibilities for misunderstanding would still exist, even if mind could speak to mind? These are only a few of the questions that have been considered. And in the pages that follow, you will find some of the most diverting and ingenious answers yet conceived.

—Robert Silverberg

The Mindworm

●
●
●

BY C. M. KORNBLUTH

The late Cyril Kornbluth was not an optimistic man, and in his science fiction he often took a bleak view of humanity's future, as well as of its past and its present. Telepathy, as he portrays it in this chilling and unforgettable story, is no gateway to warm understanding— but merely the means of sustenance for a strange, repellent kind of vampire.

*T*he handsome j.g. and the pretty nurse held out against it as long as they reasonably could, but blue Pacific water, languid tropical nights and the low atoll dreaming on the horizon—and the complete absence of any other nice young people for company on the small, uncomfortable parts boat—did their work. On June 30th they watched through dark glasses as the dazzling thing burst over the fleet and the atoll. Her manicured hand gripped his arm in excitement

13

and terror. Unfelt radiation sleeted through their loins.

A storekeeper-third-class named Bielaski watched the young couple with more interest than he showed in Test Able. After all, he had twenty-five dollars riding on the nurse. That night he lost it to a chief bo'sun's mate who had backed the j.g.

In the course of time, the careless nurse was discharged under conditions other than honorable. The j.g., who didn't like to put things in writing, phoned her all the way from Manila to say it was a damned shame. When her gratitude gave way to specific inquiry, their overseas connection went bad and he had to hang up.

She had a child, a boy, turned it over to a foundling home and vanished from his life into a series of good jobs and finally marriage.

The boy grew up stupid, puny and stubborn, greedy and miserable. To the home's hilarious young athletics director he suddenly said: "You hate me. You think I make the rest of the boys look bad."

The athletics director blustered and laughed, and later told the doctor over coffee: "I watch myself around the kids. They're sharp—they catch a look or a gesture and it's like a blow in the face to them; I know that, so I watch myself. So how did he know?"

The doctor told the boy: "Three pounds more this month isn't bad, but how about you pitch in and clean up your plate *every* day? Can't live on meat and water; those vegetables make you big and strong."

The boy said: "What's 'neurasthenic' mean?"

The doctor later said to the director: "It made my flesh creep. I was looking at his little spindling body and dishing out the old pep-talk about growing big and strong, and inside my head I was thinking, 'We'd call him neurasthenic in the old days,' and then out he popped with it. What should we do? Should we do anything? Maybe it'll go away. I don't know anything about these things. I don't know whether anybody does."

"Reads minds, does he?" asked the director. *Be damned if he's going to read my mind about Schultz Meat Market's ten per cent.* "Doctor, I think I'm going to take my vacation a little early this year. Has anybody shown any interest in adopting the child?"

"Not him. He wasn't a baby-doll when we got him, and at present he's an exceptionally unattractive-looking kid. You know how people don't give a damn about anything but their looks."

"*Some* couples would take anything, or so they tell me."

"Unapproved for foster-parenthood, you mean?"

"Red tape and arbitrary classifications sometimes limit us too severely in our adoptions."

"If you're going to wish him on some screwball couple that the courts turned down as unfit, I want no part of it."

"You don't have to have any part of it, doctor. By the way, which dorm does he sleep in?"

"West," grunted the doctor, leaving the office.

The director called a few friends—a judge, a couple the judge referred him to, a court clerk. Then he left by way of the east wing of the building.

The boy survived three months with the Berrymans. Hard-drinking Mimi alternately caressed and shrieked at him; Edward W. tried to be a good scout and just gradually lost interest, looking clean through him. He hit the road in June and got by with it for a while. He wore a Boy Scout uniform, and Boy Scouts can turn up anywhere, anytime. The money he had taken with him lasted a month. When the last penny of the last dollar was three days spent, he was adrift on a Ne-braska prairie. He had walked out of the last small town because the constable was beginning to wonder what on earth he was hanging around for and whom he belonged to. The town was miles behind on the two-lane highway; the infrequent cars did not stop.

One of Nebraska's "rivers," a dry bed at this time of year, lay ahead, spanned by a railroad culvert. There were some men in its shade, and he was hungry.

They were ugly, dirty men, and their thoughts were muddled and stupid. They called him "Shorty" and gave him a little dirty bread and some stinking sar-dines from a can. The thoughts of one of them became less muddled and uglier. He talked to the rest out of the boy's hearing, and they whooped with laughter. The boy got ready to run, but his legs wouldn't hold him up.

He could read the thoughts of the men quite clearly as they headed for him. Outrage, fear and disgust blended in him and somehow turned inside out and one of the men was dead on the dry ground, grasshoppers vaulting onto his flannel shirt, the others backing away, frightened now, not frightening.

He wasn't hungry any more; he felt quite comfortable and satisfied. He got up and headed for the other men, who ran. The rearmost of them was thinking *Jeez he folded up the evil eye we was only gonna—*

Again the boy let the thoughts flow into his head and again he flipped his own thoughts around them; it was quite easy to do. It was different—this man's terror from the other's lustful anticipation. But both had their points. . . .

At his leisure, he robbed the bodies of three dollars and twenty-four cents.

Thereafter his fame preceded him like a death-wind. Two years on the road and he had his growth, and his fill of the dull and stupid minds he met there. He moved to northern cities, a year here, a year there, quiet, unobtrusive, prudent, an epicure.

Sebastian Long woke suddenly, with something on his mind. As night-fog cleared away he remembered, happily. Today he started the Demeter Bowl! At last there was time, at last there was money—six hundred and twenty-three dollars in the bank. He had packed and shipped the three dozen cocktail glasses last night, engraved with Mrs. Klausman's initials—his last commercial order for as many months as the Bowl would take.

He shifted from nightshirt to denims, gulped coffee, boiled an egg but was too excited to eat it. He went to the front of his shop-workroom-apartment, checked the lock, waved at neighbors' children on their way to school, and ceremoniously set a sign in the cluttered window.

It said: NO COMMERCIAL ORDERS TAKEN UNTIL FURTHER NOTICE.

From a closet he tenderly carried a shrouded object that made a double armful and laid it on his workbench. Unshrouded, it was a glass bowl—*what* a glass bowl! The clearest Swedish lead glass, the purest lines he had ever seen, his secret treasure since the crazy day he had bought it, long ago, for six months' earnings. His wife had given him hell for that until the day she died. From the closet he brought a portfolio filled with sketches and designs dating back to the day he had bought the bowl. He smiled over the first, excitedly scrawled—a florid, rococo conception, unsuited to the classicism of the lines and the serenity of the perfect glass.

Through many years and hundreds of sketches he had refined his conception to the point where it was, he humbly felt, not unsuited to the medium. A strongly molded Demeter was to dominate the piece, a matron as serene as the glass, and all the fruits of the earth would flow from her gravely outstretched arms.

Suddenly and surely, he began to work. With a candle he thinly smoked an oval area on the outside of the bowl. Two steady fingers clipped the Demeter drawing against the carbon black; a hair-fine needle in his other hand traced her lines. When the transfer of the design was done, Sebastian Long readied his lathe. He fitted a small copper wheel, slightly worn as he liked them, into the chuck and with his fingers charged it with the finest rouge from Rouen. He took an ashtray cracked in delivery and held it against the spinning disk. It bit in smoothly, with the *wiping* feel to it that was exactly right.

Holding out his hands, seeing that the fingers did not tremble with excitement, he eased the great bowl to the lathe and was about to make the first tiny cut of the millions that would go into the masterpiece.

Somebody knocked on his door and rattled the doorknob.

Sebastian Long did not move or look toward the door. Soon the busybody would read the sign and go away. But the pounding and the rattling of the knob went on. He eased down the bowl and angrily went to the window, picked up the sign and shook it at who-ever it was—he couldn't make out the face very well. But the idiot wouldn't go away.

The engraver unlocked the door, opened it a bit and snapped: "The shop is closed. I shall not be taking any orders for several months. Please don't bother me now."

"It's about the Demeter Bowl," said the intruder.

Sebastian Long stared at him. "What the devil do you know about my Demeter Bowl?" He saw the man was a stranger, undersized by a little, middle-aged. . . .

"Just let me in, please," urged the man. "It's important. Please!"

"I don't know what you're talking about," said the
engraver. "But what do you know about my Demeter
Bowl?" He hooked his thumbs pugnaciously over the
waistband of his denims and glowered at the stranger.
The stranger promptly took advantage of his hand
being removed from the door and glided in.

Sebastian Long thought briefly that it might be a
nightmare as the man darted quickly about his shop,
picking up a graver and throwing it down, picking up a
wire scratch-wheel and throwing it down. "Here, you!"
he roared, as the stranger picked up a crescent wrench
which he did not throw down.

As Long started for him, the stranger darted to the
workbench and brought the crescent wrench down
shatteringly on the bowl.

Sebastian Long's heart was bursting with sorrow
and rage; such a storm of emotions as he never had
known thundered through him. Paralyzed, he saw the
stranger smile with anticipation.

The engraver's legs folded under him and he fell
to the floor, drained and dead.

The Mindworm, locked in the bedroom of his brownstone front, smiled again, reminiscently.

Smiling, he checked the day on a wall calendar.

"Dolores!" yelled her mother in Spanish. "Are you
going to pass the whole day in there?"

She had been practicing low-lidded, sexy half-smiles

like Lauren Bacall in the bathroom mirror. She stormed out and yelled in English: "I don't know how many times I tell you not to call me that Spick name no more!"

"Dolly!" sneered her mother. "Dah-lee! When was there a Saint Dah-lee that you call yourself after, eh?"

The girl snarled a Spanish obscenity at her mother and ran down the tenement stairs. Jeez, she was gonna be late for sure!

Held up by a stream of traffic between her and her streetcar, she danced with impatience. Then the miracle happened. Just like in the movies, a big convertible pulled up before her and its lounging driver said, opening the door: "You seem to be in a hurry. Could I drop you somewhere?"

Dazed at the sudden realization of a hundred daydreams, she did not fail to give the driver a low-lidded, sexy smile as she said: "Why, *thanks!*" and climbed in. He wasn't no Cary Grant, but he had all his hair . . . kind of small, but so was she . . . and jeez, the convertible had *leopard-skin seat covers!*

The car was in the stream of traffic, purring down the avenue. "It's a lovely day," she said. "Really too nice to work."

The driver smiled shyly, kind of like Jimmy Stewart but of course not so tall, and said: "I feel like playing hooky myself. How would you like a spin down Long Island?"

"Be wonderful!" The convertible cut left on an odd-numbered street.

"Play hooky, you said. What do you do?"

"Advertising."

"Advertising!" Dolly wanted to kick herself for ever having doubted, for ever having thought in low, self-loathing moments that it wouldn't work out, that she'd marry a grocer or a mechanic and live forever after in a smelly tenement and grow old and sick and stooped. She felt vaguely in her happy daze that it might have been cuter, she might have accidentally pushed him into a pond or something, but this was cute enough. An advertising man, leopard-skin seat covers . . . what more could a girl with a sexy smile and a nice little figure want?

Speeding down the South Shore she learned that his name was Michael Brent, exactly as it ought to be. She wished she could tell him she was Jennifer Brown or one of those real cute names they had nowadays, but was reassured when he told her he thought Dolly Gonzalez was a beautiful name. He didn't, and she noticed the omission, add: "It's the most beautiful name I ever heard!" That, she comfortably thought as she settled herself against the cushions, would come later.

They stopped at Medford for lunch, a wonderful lunch in a little restaurant where you went down some steps and there were candles on the table. She called him "Michael" and he called her "Dolly." She learned that he liked dark girls and thought the stories in *True Story* really were true, and that he thought she was just tall enough, and that Greer Garson was wonderful, but not the way she was, and that he thought her dress was just wonderful.

They drove slowly after Medford, and Michael Brent did most of the talking. He had traveled all over the world. He had been in the war and wounded—just a flesh wound. He was 38, and had been married once, but she died. There were no children. He was alone in the world. He had nobody to share his town house in the 50's, his country place in Westchester, his lodge in the Maine woods. Every word sent the girl floating higher and higher on a tide of happiness; the signs were unmistakable.

When they reached Montauk Point, the last sandy bit of the continent before blue water and Europe, it was sunset, with a great wrinkled sheet of purple and rose stretching half across the sky and the first stars appearing above the dark horizon of the water.

The two of them walked from the parked car out onto the sand, alone, bathed in glorious Technicolor. Her heart was nearly bursting with joy as she heard Michael Brent say, his arms tightening around her: "Darling, will you marry me?"

"Oh, *yes* Michael!" she breathed, dying.

The Mindworm, drowsing, suddenly felt the sharp sting of danger. He cast out through the great city, dragging tentacles of thought:

". . . die if she don't let me . . ."

". . . six an' six is twelve an' carry one an' three is four . . ."

". . . gobblegobble madre de dios pero soy gobble-gobble . . ."

"... parlay Domino an' Missab and shoot the roll on Duchess Peg in the feature ..."

"... melt resin add the silver chloride and dissolve in oil of lavender stand and decant and fire to cone 012 give you shimmering streaks of luster down the walls ..."

"... moiderin' square-headed gobblegobble tried ta poke his eye out wassamatta witta ref ..."

"... O God I am most heartily sorry I have offended thee in ..."

"... talk like a commie ..."

"... gobblegobblegobble two dolla twenny-fi' sense gobble ..."

"... just a nip and fill it up with water and brush my teeth ..."

"... really know I'm God but fear to confess their sins ..."

"... dirty lousy rock-headed claw-handed paddle-footed goggle-eyed snot-nosed hunch-backed feeble-minded pot-bellied son of ..."

"... write on the wall alfie is a stunkur and then ..."

"... thinks I believe it's a television set but I know he's got a bomb in there but who can I tell who can help so alone ..."

"... gabble was ich weiss nicht gabble geh bei Broadway gabble ..."

"... habt mein daughter Rosie such a fella gobble-gobble ..."

"... wonder if that's one didn't look back ..."

"... seen with her in the Medford restaurant ..."

The Mindworm struck into that thought.

"...not a mark on her but the M. E.'s have been wrong before and heart failure don't mean a thing anyway try to talk to her old lady authorize an autopsy get Pancho little guy talks Spanish be best . . ."

The Mindworm knew he would have to be moving again—soon. He was sorry; some of the thoughts he had tapped indicated good . . . hunting?

Regretfully, he again dragged his net:

"... with chartreuse drinks I mean drapes could use a drink come to think of it . . ."

"... reep-beep-reep-beep reepiddy-beepiddy-beep bop man wadda beat . . ."

"$\Delta^2\psi_n + 8\dfrac{\pi^2\mu}{h^2}(E_n + \dfrac{e^2Z}{r})\,\psi_n = 0$." *What the Hell was that?*

The Mindworm withdrew, in frantic haste. The intelligence was massive, its overtones those of a vigorous adult. He had learned from certain dangerous children that there was peril of a leveling flow. Shaken and scared, he contemplated traveling. He would need more than that wretched girl had supplied, and it would not be epicurean. There would be no time to find individuals at a ripe emotional crisis, or goad them to one. It would be plain—munching. The Mindworm drank a glass of water, also necessary to his metabolism.

EIGHT FOUND DEAD
IN UPTOWN MOVIE;
"MOLESTER" SOUGHT

Eight persons, including three women, were found

dead Wednesday night of unknown causes in widely separated seats in the balcony of the Odeon Theater at 117th St. and Broadway. Police are seeking a man described by the balcony usher, Michael Fenelly, 18, as "acting like a woman-molester."

Fenelly discovered the first of the fatalities after seeing the man "moving from one empty seat to another several times." He went to ask a woman in a seat next to one the man had just vacated whether he had annoyed her. She was dead.

Almost at once, a scream rang out. In another part of the balcony Mrs. Sadie Rabinowitz, 40, uttered the cry when another victim toppled from his seat next to her.

Theater manager I. J. Marcusohn stopped the show and turned on the house lights. He tried to instruct his staff to keep the audience from leaving before the police arrived. He failed to get word to them in time, however, and most of the audience was gone when a detail from the 24th Pct. and an ambulance from Harlem hospital took over at the scene of the tragedy.

The Medical Examiner's office has not yet made a report as to the causes of death. A spokesman said the victims showed no signs of poisoning or violence. He added that it "was inconceivable that it could be a coincidence."

Lt. John Braidwood of the 24th Pct. said of the alleged molester: "We got a fair description of him and naturally we will try to bring him in for questioning."

Clickety-click, clickety-click, clickety-click sang the rails as the Mindworm drowsed in his coach seat.

Some people were walking forward from the diner. One was thinking: "Different-looking fellow. (a) he's aberrant. (b) he's nonaberrant and ill. Cancel (b)—respiration normal, skin smooth and healthy, no tremor of limbs, well-groomed. Is aberrant (1) trivially. (2) significantly. Cancel (1)—displayed no involuntary interest when . . . odd! *Running* for the washroom! Unexpected because (a) neat grooming indicates amour propre inconsistent with amusing others; (b) evident health inconsistent with . . ." It had taken one second, was fully detailed.

The Mindworm, locked in the toilet of the coach, wondered what the next stop was. He was getting off at it—not frightened, just careful. Dodge them, keep dodging them and everything would be all right. Send out no mental taps until the train was far away and everything would be all right.

He got off at a West Virginia coal and iron town surrounded by ruined mountains and filled with the offscourings of Eastern Europe. Serbs, Albanians, Croats, Hungarians, Slovenes, Bulgarians and all possible combinations and permutations thereof. He walked slowly from the smoke-stained, brownstone passenger station. The train had roared on its way.

". . . ain' no gemmum that's fo sho', fi-cen' tip fo' a good shine lak ah give um . . ."

". . . dumb bassar don't know how to make out a billa lading yet he ain't never gonna know so fire him get it over with . . ."

". . . gabblegabblegabble . . ." Not a word he recognized in it.

"... gobblegobble dat tam vooman I brek she nack ..."

"... gobble trink visky chin glassabeer gobblegobblegobble ..."

"... gabblegabblegabble ..."

"... makes me so gobblegobble mad little no-good tramp no she ain' but I don' like no standup from no dame ..."

A blond, square-headed boy fuming under a street light.

"... out wit' Casey Oswiak I could kill that dumb bohunk alla time trine ta paw her ..."

It was a possibility. The Mindworm drew near.

"... stand me up for that gobblegobble bohunk I oughtta slap her inna mush like my ole man says ..."

"Hello," said the Mindworm.

"Waddaya wan'?"

"Casey Oswiak told me to tell you not to wait up for your girl. He's taking her out tonight."

The blond boy's rage boiled into his face and shot from his eyes. He was about to swing when the Mindworm began to feed. It was like pheasant after chicken, venison after beef. The coarseness of the environment, or the ancient strain? The Mindworm wondered as he strolled down the street. A girl passed him:

"... oh but he's gonna be mad like last time wish I came right away so jealous kinda nice but he might bust me one some day be nice to him tonight there he is lam'post leaning on it looks kinda funny gawd I hope he ain't drunk looks kinda funny sleeping sick or bozhe moi gabblegabblegabble ..."

Her thoughts trailed into a foreign language of which the Mindworm knew not a word. After hysteria had gone she recalled, in the foreign language, that she had passed him.

The Mindworm, stimulated by the unfamiliar quality of the last feeding, determined to stay for some days. He checked in at a Main Street hotel.

Musing, he dragged his net:

"... gobblegobble whomp year gobblecheskygobble-gabblechyesh ..."

"... take him down cellar beat the can off the damn chesky thief put the fear of god into him teach him can't bust into no boxcars in *mah* parta the caounty ..."

"... gabblegabble ..."

"... phone ole Mister Ryan in She-cawgo and he'll tell them three-card monte grifters who got the horse-room rights in this necka the woods by damn don't pay protection money for no protection ..."

The Mindworm followed that one further; it sounded as though it could lead to some money if he wanted to stay in the town long enough.

The Eastern Europeans of the town, he mistakenly thought, were like the tramps and bums he had known and fed on during his years on the road—stupid and safe, safe and stupid, quite the same thing.

In the morning he found no mention of the square-headed boy's death in the town's paper and thought it had gone practically unnoticed. It had—by the paper, which was of, by and for the coal and iron company and its native-American bosses and straw bosses. The other town, the one without a charter or police force, with only an imported weekly newspaper or two from the nearest city, noticed it. The other town had roots more than two thousand years deep, which are hard to pull up. But the Mindworm didn't know it was there.

He fed again that night, on a giddy young street-walker in her room. He had astounded and delighted her with a fistful of ten-dollar bills before he began to gorge. Again the delightful difference from city-bred folk was there. . . .

Again in the morning he had been unnoticed, he thought. The chartered town, unwilling to admit that there were streetwalkers or that they were found dead, wiped the slate clean; its only member who really cared was the native-American cop on the beat who had collected weekly from the dead girl.

The other town, unknown to the Mindworm, buzzed with it. A delegation went to the other town's only public officer. Unfortunately he was young, American-trained, perhaps even ignorant about some important things. For what he told them was: "My children, that is foolish superstition. Go home."

The Mindworm, through the day, roiled the surface of the town proper by allowing himself to be roped into a poker game in a parlor of the hotel. He wasn't good at it, he didn't like it, and he quit with relief when he had cleaned six shifty-eyed, hard-drinking loafers out of about three hundred dollars. One of them went straight to the police station and accused the unknown of being a sharper. A humorous sergeant, the Mindworm was pleased to note, joshed the loafer out of his temper.

Nightfall again, hunger again. . . .

He walked the streets of the town and found them empty. It was strange. The native-American citizens were out, tending bar, walking their beats, locking up their newspaper on the stones, collecting their rents, managing their movies—but where were the others? He cast his net:

". . . gobblegobblegobble whomp year gobble . . ."

". . . crazy old Pollack mama of mine try to lock me in with Errol Flynn at the Majestic never know the difference if I sneak out the back . . ."

That was near. He crossed the street and it was nearer. He homed on the thought:

". . . jeez he's a hunka man like Stanley but he never looks at me that Vera Kowalik I'd like to kick her just once in the gobblegobblegobble crazy old mama won't be American so ashamed . . ."

It was half a block, no more, down a side street. Brick houses, two stories, with back yards on an alley. She was going out the back way.

How strangely quiet it was in the alley.

". . . ea-sy down them steps fix that damn board that's how she caught me last time what the hell are they all so scared of went to see Father Drugas won't talk bet somebody got it again that Vera Kowalik and her big . . ."

". . . gobble bozhe gobble whomp year gobble . . ."

She was closer; she was closer.

"All think I'm a kid show them who's a kid bet if
Stanley caught me all alone out here in the alley dark
and all he wouldn't think I was a kid that damn Vera
Kowalik her folks don't think she's a kid . . ."

For all her bravado she was stark terrified when he
said: "Hello."

"Who—who—who—?" she stammered.

Quick, before she screamed. Her terror was delightful.

Not too replete to be alert, he cast about, questing.

". . . gobblegobblegobble whomp year."

The countless eyes of the other town, with more
than two thousand years of experience in such things,
had been following him. What he had sensed as a
meaningless hash of noise was actually an impas-
sioned outburst in a nearby darkened house.

"Fools! fools! Now he has taken a virgin! I said not
to wait. What will we say to her mother?"

An old man with handlebar mustache and, in spite
of the heat, his shirt sleeves decently rolled down and
buttoned at the cuffs, evenly replied: "My heart in me
died with hers, Casimir, but one must be sure. It
would be a terrible thing to make a mistake in such an
affair."

The weight of conservative elder opinion was with
him. Other old men with mustaches, some perhaps re-
membering mistakes long ago, nodded and said: "A
terrible thing. A terrible thing."

The Mindworm strolled back to his hotel and napped

on the made bed briefly. A tingle of danger awakened him. Instantly he cast out:

"... gobblegobble whompyear."

"... whampyir."

"WAMPYIR!"

Close! Close and deadly!

The door of his room burst open, and mustached old men with their shirt sleeves rolled down and decently buttoned at the cuffs unhesitatingly marched in, their thoughts a turmoil of alien noises, foreign gibberish that he could not wrap his mind around, disconcerting, from every direction.

The sharpened stake was through his heart and the scythe blade through his throat before he could realize that he had not been the first of his kind; and that what clever people have not yet learned, some quite ordinary people have not yet entirely forgotten.

Psyclops

BY BRIAN W. ALDISS

In this elegant little story, the celebrated British master of science fiction, Brian Aldiss, investigates two aspects of telepathy simultaneously: communication across vast gulfs of space, and communication across that even greater gulf that separates the born from the unborn.

*M*mmm I.

First statement: I am I. I am everything. Everything, everywhere.

The universe is constructed of me, I am the whole of it. Am I? What is that throbbing that is not of me? That must be me too; after a while I shall understand it. All now is dim. Dim mmmm.

Even I am dim. In all this great strangeness and darkness of me, in all this universe of me, I am shadow. A memory of me. Could I be a memory of . . . not—me? Paradox: if I am everything, could there be a not-me?

Why am I having thoughts? Why am I not, as I was before, just mmmm?

Wake up! It's urgent!

No! Deny it! I am the universe. If you can speak to me you must be me, so I command you to be still. There must be only the soothing mmmm.

. . . you are not the universe! Listen!

Louder?

Can you hear at last?

Non-comprehension. I must be everything. Can there be a part of me, like the throbbing, which is . . . separate?

Am I getting through? Answer!

Who . . . are you?

Do not be frightened.

Are you another . . . universe?

I am not a universe. You are not a universe. You are in danger and I must help you.

Mmmm. Must be mmmm. . . .

. . . If only there were a psychofetalist within light-years of here. . . . Well, keep trying. Wake up! You must wake up to survive!

Who are you?

I am your father.

Non-comprehension. Are you the throbbing which is not me?

No. I am a long way from you. Light-years away.

You bring me feelings of . . . pain.

Don't be afraid of it, but know there is much pain all about you. I am in constant pain.

Interest.

Good! First things first. You are most important.

I know that. All this is not happening. Somehow I catch these echoes, these dreams.

Try to concentrate. You are only one of millions like you. You and I are of the same species: human beings. I am born, you are unborn.

Meaningless.

Listen! Your "universe" is inside another human being. Soon you will emerge into the real universe.

Still meaningless. Curious.

Keep alert. I will send you pictures to help you understand. . . .

Uh. . . ? Distance? Sight? Color? Form? Definitely do not like this. Frightened. Frightened of falling, insecure. . . . Must immediately retreat to safe mmmm. Mmmm.

Better let him rest! After all, he's only six months; at the Pre-natal Academies they don't begin rousing and education till seven and a half months. And then they're trained to the job. If only I knew—my leg, you blue swine!

That picture . . .

Well done! I'm really sorry to rouse you so early, but it's vital.

Praise for me, warm feelings. Good. Better than being alone in the universe.

That's a great step forward, son. I can almost realize how the Creator felt, when you say that.

Non-comprehension.

Sorry, my fault; let the thought slip by. Must be

careful. You were going to ask me about the picture I sent you. Shall I send again?

Only a little at once. Curious. Shape, color, beauty. Is that the real universe?

That was just Earth I showed you, where I was born, where I hope you will be born.

Non-comprehension. Show again . . . shapes, tones, scents. . . . Ah, this time not so strange. Different?

Yes, a different picture. Many pictures of Earth. Look.

Ah. . . . Better than my darkness. . . . I know only my darkness, sweet and warm, yet I seem to remember those—trees.

That's a race memory, son. Your faculties are beginning to work, now.

More beautiful pictures please.

We cannot waste too long on the pictures. I've got a lot to tell you before you get out of range. These blue devils—

Why do you cease sending so abruptly? Hello? . . . Nothing. Father? . . . Nothing. Was there ever anything, or have I been alone and dreaming?

Nothing in all my universe but the throbbing. Is someone here with me? No, no answer. I must ask the voice, if the voice comes back. Now I must mmmm. Am no longer content as I was before. Strange feelings. . . . I want more pictures; I want . . . to . . .

Mmmm.

Dreaming myself to be a fish, fin-tailed, flickering

through deep, still water. All is green and warm and without menace, and I swim forever with assurance. . . . And then the water splits into lashing cords and plunges down, down, down a sunlit cliff. I fight to turn back, carried forward, fighting to return to the deep, sure dark—

—if you want to save yourself! Wake if you want to save yourself! I can't hold out much longer. Another few days across these mountains—

Go away! Leave me to myself. I can have nothing to do with you.

You must try and understand! I know it's agony for you, but you must stir yourself and take in what I say. It is imperative.

Nothing is imperative here. And now my mind seems to clear. Yes! I exist in the darkness where formerly there was nothing. Yes, there are imperatives, that I can recognize. Father?

What are you trying to say?

Confused. Understanding better, trying harder, but so confused.

Do not worry about that. It is your twin sister. The Pollux II hospital diagnosed twins, one boy and one girl.

So many concepts I cannot grasp. I should despair but for curiosity prodding me on. I'm one of a pair?

There you have it. That is a little girl lying next to you: you can hear her heart beating. Your mother—

Stop, stop! Too much to understand at once. Must think to myself about this.

*Keep calm. There is something you must do for me
—for us all. If you do that, there is no danger.*

Tell me quickly.

*As yet it is too difficult. In a few days you will be
ready—if I can hang on that long.*

Why is it difficult?

Only because you are small.

Where are you?

*I am on a world like Earth which is ninety light-
years from Earth and getting farther from you even as
we communicate together.*

Why? How? Don't understand. So much is now beyond my understanding; before you came everything
was peaceful and dim.

*Lie quiet and don't fret, son. You're doing well; you
take the points quickly, you'll reach Earth yet. You are
traveling toward Earth in a spaceship which left
Mirone, planet where I am, sixteen days ago.*

Send that picture of a spaceship again.

Coming up. . . .

It is a kind of enclosure for us all. That idea I can
more or less grasp, but you don't explain distances to
me satisfactorily.

*These are big distances, what we call light-years. I
can't picture them for you properly because a human
mind never really grasps them.*

Then they don't exist.

*Unfortunately they exist all right. But they are only
comprehensible as mathematical concepts. OHHH!
My leg. . . .*

Why are you stopping? I remember you suddenly stopped before. You send a horrible pain thought, then you are gone. Answer.

Wait a minute.

I can hardly hear you. Now I am interested, why do you not continue? Are you there?

. . . this is all beyond me. We're all finished. Judy, my love, if only I could reach you. . . .

Who are you talking to? This is frustrating. You are so faint and your message so blurred.

Call you when I can. . . .

Fear and pain. Only symbols from his mind to mine, yet they have an uncomfortable meaning of their own—something elusive. Perhaps another race memory.

My own memory is not good. Un-used. I must train it. Something he said eludes me; I must try and remember it. Yet why should I bother? None of it really concerns me, I am safe here, safe forever in this darkness. This whole thing is imagination. I am talking to myself. Wait! I can feel projections coming back again. Do not trouble to listen. Curious.

. . . gangrene, without doubt. Shall be dead before these blue devils get me to their village. So much Judy and I planned to do. . . .

Are you listening, son?

No, no.

Listen carefully while I give you instructions.

Have something to ask you.

Please save it. The connection between us is growing attenuated; soon we will be out of mind range.

Indifferent.

My dear child, how could you be other than indifferent! I am truly sorry to have broken so early into your fetal sleep.

An unnamable sensation, half-pleasant: gratitude, love? No doubt a race memory.

It may be so. Try to remember me—later. Now, business. Your mother and I were on our way back to Earth when we stopped on this world Mirone, where I now am. It was an unnecessary luxury to break our journey. How bitterly now I wish we had never stopped.

Why did you?

Well, it was chiefly to please Judy—your mother. This is a beautiful world, around the North Pole, anyhow. We had wandered some way from the ship when a group of natives burst out upon us.

Natives?

People who live here. They are sub-human, blue-skinned and hairless—not pretty to look at.

Picture!

I think you'd be better without one. Judy and I ran for the ship. We were nearly up to it when a rock caught me behind the knee—they were pitching rocks at us—and I went down. Judy never noticed until she was in the air-lock, and then the savages were on me. My leg was hurt; I couldn't even put up a fight.

Please tell me no more of this. I want mmmm.

Listen, son! That's all the frightening part. The savages are taking me over the mountains to their village. I don't think they mean to harm me; I'm just a . . . curiosity to them.

Please let me mmmm.

You can go comatose as soon as I've explained how these little spacecraft work. Astrogating, the business of getting from one planet to another, is far too intricate a task for anyone but an expert to master. I'm not an expert; I'm a geohistorian. So the whole thing is done by a robot pilot. You feed it details like payload, gravities and destination, and it juggles them with the data in its memory banks and works out all the course for you—carries you home safely, in fact. Do you get all that?

This sounds complicated.

Now you're talking like your mother, boy. She's never bothered, but actually it's all simple; the complications take place under the steel paneling where you don't worry about them. The point I'm trying to make is that steering is all automatic once you've punched in a few co-ordinates.

I'm tired.

So am I. Fortunately, before we left the ship that last time, I had set up the figures for Earth. OK?

If you had not, she would not have been able to get home?

Exactly it. Keep trying! She left Mirone safely and you are now heading for Earth—but you'll never make it. When I set the figures up, they were right; but my not being aboard made them wrong. Every split second of thrust the ship makes is calculated for an extra weight that isn't there. It's here with me, being hauled along a mountain.

Is this bad? Does it mean we reach Earth too fast?

No, son. IT MEANS YOU'LL NEVER REACH EARTH AT ALL. The ship moves in a hyperbola, and although my weight is only about one eight-thousandth of total ship's mass, that tiny fraction of error will have multiplied itself into a couple of light-years by the time you get adjacent to the solar system.

I'm trying, but this talk of distance means nothing to me. Explain it again.

Where you are there is neither light nor space; how do I make you feel what a light-year is? No, you'll just have to take it from me that the crucial point is, you'll shoot right past the Earth.

Can't we go on?

You will—if nothing is done about it. But landfall will be delayed some thousands of years.

You are growing fainter. Strain too much. Must mmmm.

The fish again, and the water. No peace in the pool now. Cool pool, cruel pool, pool. . . . The waters whirl toward the brink.

I am the fish-fetus. Have I dreamed? Was there a voice talking to me? It seems unlikely. Something I had to ask it, one gigantic fact which made nonsense of everything; something—cannot remember.

Perhaps there was no voice. Perhaps in this darkness I have taken a wrong choice between sanity and non-sanity.

. . . thank heavens for hot spring water. . . .

Hello! Father?

How long will they let me lie here in this pool? They must realize I'm not long for this world, or any other.

I'm awake and answering!

Just let me lie here. Son, it's man's first pleasure and his last to lie and swill in hot water. Wish I could live to know you. . . . However. Here's what you have to do.

Am powerless here. Unable to do anything.

Don't get frightened. There's something you already do very expertly—telemit.

Non-comprehension.

We talk to each other over this growing distance by what is called telepathy. It's part gift, part skill. It happens to be the only contact between distant planets, except spaceships. But whereas spaceships take time to get anywhere, thought is instantaneous.

Understood.

Good. Unfortunately, whereas spaceships get anywhere in time, thought has a definite limited range. Its span is as strictly governed as—well, as the size of a plant, for instance. When you are fifty light-years from Mirone, contact between us will abruptly cease.

How far apart are we now?

At the most we have forty-eight hours more in contact.

Don't leave me. I shall be lonely!

I'll be lonely too—but not for long. But you, son, you are already halfway to Earth, or as near as I can estimate it, you are. As soon as contact between us ceases, you must call TRE.

Which means?

Telepath Radial Earth. It's a general control and information center, permanently beamed for any sort of emergency. You can raise them. I can't.

They won't know me.

I'll give you their call pattern. They'll soon know you when you telemit. You can give them my pattern for identification if you like. You must explain what is happening.

Will they believe?

Of course.

Are they real?

Of course. Tell TRE what the trouble is; they'll send out a fast ship to pick Judy and you up before you are out of range.

I want to ask you—

Wait a minute, son. . . . You're getting faint . . . Can you smell the gangrene over all those light-years? . . . These blue horrors are lifting me out of the spring, and I'll probably pass out. Not much time . . .

Pain. Pain and silence. All like a dream.

. . . distance . . .

Father! Louder!

. . . too feeble. . . . Done all I could. . . .

Why did you rouse me and not communicate with my mother?

The village! We're nearly there. Just down the valley and then it's journey's end . . . Human race only developing telepathic powers gradually . . . Steady, you fellows!

The question, answer the question.

That is the answer. Easy down the slope, boys, don't burst this big leg, eh? Ah . . . I have telepathic ability but Judy hasn't; I couldn't call her a yard away. But you have the ability . . . Easy there! All the matter in the universe is in my leg . . .

You sound so muddled. Has my sister this power?

Good old Mendelian theory. . . . You and your sister, one sensitive, one not. Two eyes of the giant and only one can see properly . . . the path's too steep to—whoa, Cyclops, steady, boy, or you'll put out that other eye.

Cannot understand!

Understand? My leg's a flaming torch—Steady, steady! Gently down the steep blue hill.

Father!

What's the matter?

I can't understand. Are you talking of real things?

Sorry, boy. Steady now. Touch of delirium; it's the pain. You'll be OK if you get in contact with TRE. Remember?

Yes, I remember. If only I could . . . I don't know. Mother is *real* then?

Yes. You must look after her.

And is the giant real?

The giant? What giant? You mean the giant hill. The people are climbing up the giant hill. Up to my giant leg. Goodbye, son. I've got to see a blue man about a . . . a leg . . .

Father! Wait, wait, look, see, I can move. I've just discovered I can *turn*. Father!

No answer now. Just a stream of silence. I have got to call TRE.

Plenty of time, Perhaps if I *turn* first. . . . Easy. I'm only six months, he said. Maybe I could call more easily if I was outside, in the real universe. If I turn again.

Now if I *kick*. . . .

Ah, easy now. Kick again. Good. Wonder if my legs are blue.

Kick.

Something yielding.

Kick. . . .

Novice

BY JAMES H. SCHMITZ

James Schmitz writes with warmth and charm and grace, and his stories have been delighting science-fiction readers for more than a quarter of a century. In recent years, Schmitz has won an enthusiastic following with a series of tales about a levelheaded young lady named Telzey Amberdon, who is not only an unusually bold and intelligent fifteen-year-old, but who happens to have well-developed psionic powers. The present story, published in 1962, was the first in the series, the one in which Telzey first came to suspect the presence of her telepathic gifts; and, one notes with pleasure, she has reappeared in a good many stories and novels since then.

48

I

There was, Telzey Amberdon thought, someone besides TT and herself in the garden. Not, of course, Aunt Halet, who was in the house waiting for an early visitor to arrive, and not one of the servants. Someone or something else must be concealed among the thickets of magnificently flowering native Jontarou shrubs about Telzey.

She could think of no other way to account for Tick-Tock's spooked behavior—nor, to be honest about it, for the manner in which her own nerves were acting up without visible cause this morning.

Telzey plucked a blade of grass, slipped the end between her lips and chewed it gently, her face puzzled and concerned. She wasn't ordinarily afflicted with nervousness. Fifteen years old, genius level, brown as a berry and not at all bad looking in her sunbriefs, she was the youngest member of one of Orado's most prominent families and a second-year law student at one of the most exclusive schools in the Federation of the Hub. Her physical, mental, and emotional health, she'd always been informed, was excellent. Aunt Halet's frequent cracks about the inherent instability of the genius level could be ignored; Halet's own stability seemed questionable at best.

But none of that made the present odd situation any less disagreeable. . . .

The trouble might have begun, Telzey decided, during the night, within an hour after they arrived from the spaceport at the guest house Halet had rented in Port Nichay for their vacation on Jontarou. Telzey had retired at once to her second-story bedroom with Tick-Tock, but she barely got to sleep before something awakened her again. Turning over, she discovered TT reared up before the window, her forepaws on the sill, big cat-head outlined against the star-hazed night sky, staring fixedly down into the garden.

Telzey, only curious at that point, climbed out of bed and joined TT at the window. There was nothing in particular to be seen, and if the scents and minor night-sounds which came from the garden weren't exactly what they were used to, Jontarou was after all an unfamiliar planet. What else would one expect here?

But Tick-Tock's muscular back felt tense and rigid when Telzey laid her arm across it, and except for an absentminded dig with her forehead against Telzey's shoulder, TT refused to let her attention be distracted from whatever had absorbed it. Now and then, a low, ominous rumble came from her furry throat, a half-angry, half-questioning sound. Telzey began to feel a little uncomfortable. She managed finally to coax Tick-Tock away from the window, but neither of them slept well the rest of the night. At breakfast, Aunt Halet made one of her typical nasty-sweet remarks.

"You look so fatigued, dear, as if you were under some severe mental strain . . . which, of course, you might be." With her gold-blond hair piled high on her head and her peaches-and-cream complexion, Halet looked fresh as a daisy herself . . . a malicious daisy. "Now wasn't I right in insisting to Jessamine that you needed a vacation away from that terribly intellectual school?" She smiled gently.

"Absolutely," Telzey agreed, restraining the impulse to fling a spoonful of egg yolk at her father's younger sister. Aunt Halet often inspired such impulses, but Telzey had promised her mother to avoid actual battles on the Jontarou trip, if possible. After breakfast, she went out into the back garden with Tick-Tock, who immediately walked into a thicket, camouflaged herself and vanished from sight. It seemed to add up to something. But what?

Telzey strolled about the garden a while, maintaining a pretense of nonchalant interest in Jontarou's flowers and colorful bug life. She experienced the most curious little chills of alarm from time to time, but discovered no signs of a lurking intruder, or of TT either. Then, for half an hour or more, she'd just sat cross-legged in the grass, waiting quietly for Tick-Tock to show up of her own accord. And the big lunkhead hadn't obliged.

Telzey scratched a tanned kneecap, scowling at Port Nichay's park trees beyond the garden wall. It seemed idiotic to feel scared when she couldn't even tell whether there was anything to be scared about! And, aside from that, another unreasonable feeling kept growing stronger by the minute now. This was to the effect that she should be doing some unstated but specific thing. . . .

In fact, that Tick-Tock *wanted* her to do some specific thing!

Completely idiotic!

Abruptly, Telzey closed her eyes and thought sharply, "Tick-Tock?" and waited—suddenly very angry at herself for having given in to her fancies to this extent—for whatever might happen.

She had never really established that she was able to tell, by a kind of symbolic mind-picture method, like a short waking dream, approximately what TT was thinking and feeling. Five years before, when she'd discovered Tick-Tock—an odd-looking and odder-behaved stray kitten then—in the woods near the Amberdons' summer home on Orado, Telzey had thought so. But it might never have been more than a colorful play of her imagination; and after she got into law school and grew increasingly absorbed in her studies, she almost forgot the matter again.

Today, perhaps because she was disturbed about Tick-Tock's behavior, the customary response was extraordinarily prompt. The warm glow of sunlight shining through her closed eyelids faded out quickly and was replaced by some inner darkness. In the darkness there appeared then an image of Tick-Tock sitting a little way off beside an open door in an old stone wall, green eyes fixed on Telzey. Telzey got the impression that TT was inviting her to go through the door, and, for some reason, the thought frightened her.

Again, there was an immediate reaction. The scene with Tick-Tock and the door vanished; and Telzey felt she was standing in a pitch-black room, knowing that if she moved even one step forward, something that was waiting there silently would reach out and grab her.

Naturally, she recoiled . . . and at once found herself sitting, eyes still closed and the sunlight bathing her lids, in the grass of the guest house garden.

She opened her eyes, looked around. Her heart was thumping rapidly. The experience couldn't have lasted more than four or five seconds, but it had been extremely vivid, a whole, compact little nightmare. None of her earlier experiments at getting into mental communication with TT had been like that.

It served her right, Telzey thought, for trying such a childish stunt at the moment! What she should have done at once was to make a methodical search for the foolish beast—TT was bound to be *somewhere* nearby —locate her behind her camouflage, and hang on to her then until this nonsense in the garden was explained! Talented as Tick-Tock was at blotting herself out, it usually was possible to spot her if one directed one's attention to shadow patterns. Telzey began a surreptitious study of the clusters of flowering bushes about her.

Three minutes later, off to her right, where the ground was banked beneath a six-foot step in the garden's terraces, Tick-Tock's outline suddenly caught her eye. Flat on her belly, head lifted above her paws, quite motionless, TT seemed like a transparent wraith stretched out along the terrace, barely discernible even when stared at directly. It was a convincing illusion; but what seemed to be rocks, plant leaves, and sunsplotched earth seen through the wraith-outline was simply the camouflage pattern TT had printed for the moment on her hide. She could have changed it completely in an instant to conform to a different background.

Telzey pointed an accusing finger.

"See you!" she announced, feeling a surge of relief which seemed as unaccountable as the rest of it.

The wraith twitched one ear in acknowledgment, the head outlines shifting as the camouflaged face turned towards Telzey. Then the inwardly uncamouflaged, very substantial-looking mouth opened slowly, showing Tick-Tock's red tongue and curved white tusks. The mouth stretched in a wide yawn, snapped shut with a click of meshing teeth, became indistinguishable again. Next, a pair of camouflaged lids drew back from TT's round, brilliant-green eyes. The eyes stared across the lawn at Telzey.

Telzey said irritably, "Quit clowning around, TT!"

The eyes blinked, and Tick-Tock's natural bronze-brown color suddenly flowed over her head, down her neck and across her body into legs and tail. Against the side of the terrace, as if materializing into solidity at that moment, appeared two hundred pounds of supple, rangy, long-tailed cat . . . or catlike creature.

TT's actual origin had never been established. The best guesses were that what Telzey had found playing around in the woods five years ago was either a biostructural experiment which had got away from a private laboratory on Orado, or some spaceman's lost pet, brought to the capital planet from one of the remote colonies beyond the Hub. On top of TT's head was a large, fluffy pompon of white fur, which might have looked ridiculous on another animal, but didn't on her. Even as a fat kitten, hanging head down from the side of a wall by the broad sucker pads in her paws, TT had possessed enormous dignity.

Telzey studied her, the feeling of relief fading again. Tick-Tock, ordinarily the most restful and composed of companions, definitely was still tensed up about something. That big, lazy yawn a moment ago, the attitude of stretched-out relaxation . . . all pure sham!

"What *is* eating you?" she asked in exasperation.

The green eyes stared at her, solemn, watchful, seeming for the fleeting instant quite alien. And why, Telzey thought, should the old question of what Tick-Tock really was pass through her mind just now? After her rather alarming rate of growth began to taper off last year, nobody had cared any more. She was simply Tick-Tock. . . .

For a moment, Telzey had the uncanny certainty of having had the answer to this situation almost in her grasp. An answer which appeared to involve the world of Jontarou, Tick-Tock, and of all unlikely factors . . . Aunt Halet.

She shook her head. TT's impassive green eyes blinked.

Jontarou? The planet lay outside Telzey's sphere of personal interests, but she'd read up on it on the way here from Orado. Among all the worlds of the Hub,

Jontarou was *the* paradise for zoologists and sportsmen, a gigantic animal preserve, its continents and
seas swarming with magnificent game. Under Federation law, it was being retained deliberately in the
primitive state in which it had been discovered. Port
Nichay, the only city, actually the only inhabited point
on Jontarou, was beautiful and quiet, a pattern of vast
but elegantly slender towers, each separated from the
others by four or five miles of rolling parkland and in-
terconnected only by the threads of transparent sky-
ways. Near the horizon, just visible from the garden,
rose the tallest towers of all, the green and gold spires
of the Shikaris' Club, a center of Federation affairs
and of social activity. From the aircar which brought
them across Port Nichay the evening before, Telzey
had seen occasional strings of guest houses, similar
to the one Halet had rented, nestling along the park
slopes.

Nothing very sinister about Port Nichay or green
Jontarou, surely!

Halet? That blond, slinky, would-be Machiavelli?
What could. . . ?

Telzey's eyes narrowed reflectively. There'd been a
minor occurrence—at least, it had seemed minor—just
before the spaceliner docked last night. A young
woman from one of the newscasting services had
asked for an interview with the daughter of Federation
Councilwoman Jessamine Amberdon. This happened
occasionally; and Telzey had no objections until the
newswoman's gossipy persistence in inquiring about

the "unusual pet" she was bringing to Port Nichay with her began to be annoying. TT might be somewhat unusual, but that was not a matter of general interest, and Telzey said so. Then Halet moved smoothly into the act and held forth on Tick-Tock's appearance, habits, and mysterious antecedents, in considerable detail.

Telzey had assumed that Halet was simply going out of her way to be irritating, as usual. Looking back on the incident, however, it occurred to her that the chatter between her aunt and the newscast woman had sounded oddly stilted—almost like something the two might have rehearsed.

Rehearsed for what purpose? Tick-Tock . . . Jontarou . . .

Telzey chewed gently on her lower lip. A vacation on Jontarou for the two of them and TT had been Halet's idea, and Halet had enthused about it so much that Telzey's mother at last talked her into accepting. Halet, Jessamine explained privately to Telzey, had felt they were intruders in the Amberdon family, had bitterly resented Jessamine's political honors and, more recently, Telzey's own emerging promise of brilliance. This invitation was Halet's way of indicating a change of heart. Wouldn't Telzey oblige?

So Telzey had obliged, though she took very little stock in Halet's change of heart. She wasn't, in fact, putting it past her aunt to have some involved dirty trick up her sleeve with this trip to Jontarou. Halet's mind worked like that.

So far there had been no actual indications of purposeful mischief. But logic did seem to require a connection between the various puzzling events here, especially the newscaster's rather forced-looking interest in Tick-Tock. Halet could easily have paid for that interview. Then TT's disturbed behavior during their first night in Port Nichay, and Telzey's own formless anxieties and fancies in connection with the guest house garden.

The last remained hard to explain. But Tick-Tock . . . and Halet . . . might know something about Jontarou that she didn't know.

Her mind returned to the results of the half-serious attempt she'd made to find out whether there was something Tick-Tock "wanted her to do." An open door? A darkness where somebody waited to grab her if she took even one step forward? It couldn't have had any significance. Or could it?

So you'd like to try magic, Telzey scoffed at herself. Baby games . . . How far would you have got at law school if you'd asked TT to help with your problems?

Then why had she been thinking about it again?

She shivered, because an eerie stillness seemed to settle on the garden. From the side of the terrace, TT's green eyes watched her.

Telzey had a feeling of sinking down slowly into a sunlit dream, into something very remote from law school problems.

"Should I go through the door?" she whispered.

The bronze cat-shape raised its head slowly. TT began to purr.

Tick-Tock's name had been derived in kittenhood from the manner in which she purred—a measured, oscillating sound, shifting from high to low, as comfortable and often as continuous as the unobtrusive pulse of an old clock. It was the first time, Telzey realized now, that she'd heard the sound since their arrival on Jontarou. It went on for a dozen seconds or so, then stopped. Tick-Tock continued to look at her.

It appeared to have been an expression of definite assent. . . .

The dreamlike sensation increased, hazing over Telzey's thoughts. If there was nothing to this mind-communication thing, what harm could symbols do? This time, she wouldn't let them alarm her. And if they did mean something . . .

She closed her eyes.

II

The sunglow outside faded instantly. Telzey caught a fleeting picture of the door in the wall, and knew in the same moment that she'd already passed through it.

She was not in the dark room then, but poised at the edge of a brightness which seemed featureless and without limit, spread out around her with a feeling-tone like "sea" or "sky." But it was an unquiet place. There was a sense of unseen things on all sides watching her and waiting.

Was this another form of the dark room—a trap set up in her mind? Telzey's attention did a quick shift.

She was seated in the grass again; the sunlight beyond her closed eyelids seemed to shine in quietly through rose-tinted curtains. Cautiously, she let her awareness return to the bright area; and it was still there. She had a moment of excited elation. She was controlling this! And why not? she asked herself. These things were happening in *her* mind, after all!

She would find out what they seemed to mean; but she would be in no rush to . . .

An impression as if, behind her, Tick-Tock had thought, "Now I can help again!"

Then a feeling of being swept swiftly, irresistibly forward, thrust out and down. The brightness exploded in thundering colors around her. In fright, she made the effort to snap her eyes open, to be back in the garden; but now she couldn't make it work. The colors continued to roar about her, like a confusion of excited, laughing, triumphant voices. Telzey felt caught in the middle of it all, suspended in invisible spider webs. Tick-Tock seemed to be somewhere nearby, looking on. Faithless, treacherous TT!

Telzey's mind made another wrenching effort, and there was a change. She hadn't got back into the garden, but the noisy, swirling colors were gone and she had the feeling of reading a rapidly moving microtape now, though she didn't actually see the tape.

The tape, she realized, was another symbol for what was happening, a symbol easier for her to understand. There were voices, or what might be voices, around her; on the invisible tape she seemed to be reading what they said.

A number of speakers, apparently involved in a fast, hot argument about what to do with her. Impressions flashed past. . . .

Why waste time with her? It was clear that kitten-talk was all she was capable of! . . . Not necessarily; that was a normal first step. Give her a little time! . . . But what—exasperatedly—could *such* a small-bite *possibly* know that would be of significant value?

There was a slow, blurred, awkward-seeming inter-ruption. Its content was not comprehensible to Telzey at all, but in some unmistakable manner it was defined as Tick-Tock's thought.

A pause as the circle of speakers stopped to consider whatever TT had thrown into the debate.

Then another impression . . . one that sent a shock of fear through Telzey as it rose heavily into her awareness. Its sheer intensity momentarily displaced the tape-reading symbolism. A savage voice seemed to rumble:

"Toss the tender small-bite to *me*"—malevolent crimson eyes fixed on Telzey from somewhere not far away—"and let's be done here!"

Startled, stammering protest from Tick-Tock, ac-companied by gusts of laughter from the circle. Great sense of humor these characters had, Telzey thought bitterly. That crimson-eyed thing wasn't joking at all!

More laughter as the circle caught her thought. Then a kind of majority opinion found sudden expression:

"Small-bite *is* learning! No harm to wait. . . . We'll find out quickly. . . ."

The tape ended; the voices faded; the colors went blank. In whatever jumbled-up form she'd been getting the impressions at that point—Telzey couldn't have begun to describe it—the whole thing suddenly stopped.

She found herself sitting in the grass, shaky, scared, eyes open. Tick-Tock stood beside the terrace, looking at her. An air of hazy unreality still hung about the garden.

She might have flipped! She didn't think so; but it certainly seemed possible! Otherwise . . . Telzey made an attempt to sort over what had happened.

Something *had* been in the garden! Something had been inside her mind. Something that was at home on Jontarou.

There'd been a feeling of perhaps fifty or sixty of these . . . well, beings. Alarming beings! Reckless, wild, hard . . . and that red-eyed nightmare! Telzey shuddered.

They'd contacted Tick-Tock first, during the night. TT understood them better than she could. Why? Telzey found no immediate answer.

Then Tick-Tock had tricked her into letting her mind be invaded by these beings. There must have been a very definite reason for that.

She looked over at Tick-Tock. TT looked back. Nothing stirred in Telzey's thoughts. Between *them* there was still no direct communication.

Then how had the beings been able to get through to her?

Telzey wrinkled her nose. Assuming this was real, it seemed clear that the game of symbols she'd made up between herself and TT had provided the opening. Her whole experience just now had been in the form of symbols, translating whatever occurred into something she could consciously grasp.

"Kitten-talk" was how the beings referred to the use of symbols; they seemed contemptuous of it. Never mind, Telzey told herself; they'd agreed she was learning.

The air over the grass appeared to flicker. Again she had the impression of reading words off a quickly moving, not quite visible tape.

"You're being taught and you're learning," was what she seemed to read. "The question was whether you were capable of partial understanding, as your friend insisted. Since you were, everything else that can be done will be accomplished quickly." A pause, then with a touch of approval, "You've a well-formed mind, small-bite! Odd and with incomprehensibilities, but well-formed . . ."

One of the beings, and a fairly friendly one—at least not unfriendly. Telzey framed a tentative mental question. "Who are you?"

"You'll know very soon." The flickering ended; she realized she and the question had been dismissed for the moment. She looked over at Tick-Tock again.

"Can't *you* talk to me now, TT?" she asked silently.

A feeling of hesitation.

"Kitten-talk!" was the impression that formed itself with difficulty then. It was awkward, searching, but it came unquestionably from TT. "Still learning, too, Telzey!" TT seemed half anxious, half angry. "We ..."

A sharp buzz-note reached Telzey's ears, wiping out the groping thought-impression. She jumped a little, glanced down. Her wrist-talker was signaling. For a moment, she seemed poised uncertainly between a world where unseen, dangerous-sounding beings referred to one as "small-bite" and where TT was learning to talk, and the familiar other world where wrist-communicators buzzed periodically in a matter-of-fact manner. Settling back into the more familiar world, she switched on the talker.

"Yes?" she said. Her voice sounded husky.

"Telzey, dear," Halet murmured honey-sweet from the talker, "would you come back into the house, please? The living room. We have a visitor who very much wants to meet you."

Telzey hesitated, eyes narrowing. Halet's visitor wanted to meet *her*?

"Why?" she asked.

"He has something *very* interesting to tell you, dear." The edge of triumphant malice showed for an instant, vanished in murmuring sweetness again. "So please hurry!"

"All right." Telzey stood up. "I'm coming."

"Fine, dear!" The talker went dead.

Telzey switched off the instrument, noticed that Tick-Tock had chosen to disappear meanwhile.

Flipped? She wondered, starting up towards the

house. It was clear Aunt Halet had prepared some unpleasant surprise to spring on her, which was hardly
more than normal behavior for Halet. The other business? She couldn't be certain of anything there. Leaving out TT's strange actions—which might have a
number of causes, after all—that entire string of
events could have been created inside her head. There
was no contradictory evidence so far.

But it could do no harm to take what *seemed* to have
happened at face value. Some pretty grim event might
be shaping up, in a very real way, around here. . . .

"You reason logically!" The impression now was of a
voice speaking to her, a voice that made no audible
sound. It was the same being who'd addressed her a
minute or two ago.

The two worlds between which Telzey had felt suspended seemed to glide slowly together and become
one.

"I go to law school," she explained to the being, almost absently.

Amused agreement. "So we heard."

"What do you want of me?" Telzey inquired.

"You'll know soon enough."

"Why not tell me now?" Telzey urged. It seemed
about to dismiss her again.

Quick impatience flared at her. "Kitten-pictures!
Kitten-thoughts! Kitten-talk! Too slow, too slow! YOUR
pictures—too much YOU! Wait till the . . ."

Circuits close . . . channels open . . . obstructions
clear? What *had* it said? There'd been only the blurred

image of a finicky, delicate, but perfectly normal technical operation of some kind.

". . . minutes now!" the voice concluded. A pause, then another thought tossed carelessly at her. "This is more important to you, small-bite, than to *us!*" The voice impression ended as sharply as if a communicator had snapped off.

Not *too* friendly! Telzey walked on towards the house, a new fear growing inside her . . . a fear like the awareness of a storm gathered nearby, still quiet —deadly quiet, but ready to break.

'Kitten-pictures!" a voice seemed to jeer distantly, a whispering in the park trees beyond the garden wall.

Halet's cheeks were lightly pinked; her blue eyes sparkled. She looked downright stunning, which meant to anyone who knew her that the worst side of Halet's nature was champing at the bit again. On uninformed males it had a dazzling effect, however; and Telzey wasn't surprised to find their visitor wearing a tranced expression when she came into the living room. He was a tall, outdoorsy man with a tanned, bony face, a neatly trained black mustache, and a scar down one cheek which would have seemed dashing if it hadn't been for the stupefied look. Beside his chair stood a large, clumsy instrument which might have been some kind of telecamera.

Halet performed introductions. Their visitor was Dr. Droon, a zoologist. He had been tuned in on Telzey's newscast interview on the liner the night before, and wondered whether Telzey would care to discuss Tick-Tock with him.

"Frankly, no," Telzey said.

Dr. Droon came awake and gave Telzey a surprised look. Halet smiled easily.

"My niece doesn't intend to be discourteous, doctor," she explained.

"Of course not," the zoologist agreed doubtfully.

"It's just," Halet went on, "that Telzey is a little, oh, sensitive where Tick-Tock is concerned. In her own way, she's attached to the animal. Aren't you, dear?"

"Yes," Telzey said blandly.

"Well, we hope this isn't going to disturb you too much, dear." Halet glanced significantly at Dr. Droon. "Dr. Droon, you must understand, is simply doing . . . well, there is something very important he must tell you now."

Telzey transferred her gaze back to the zoologist. Dr. Droon cleared his throat. "I, ah, understand, Miss Amberdon, that you're unaware of what kind of creature your, ah, Tick-Tock is?"

Telzey started to speak, then checked herself, frowning. She had been about to state that she knew exactly what kind of creature TT was . . . but she didn't, of course!

Or did she? She . . .

She scowled absentmindedly at Dr. Droon, biting her lip.

"Telzey!" Halet prompted gently.

"Huh?" Telzey said. "Oh . . . please go on, doctor!"

Dr. Droon steepled his fingers. "Well," he said, "she —your pet—is, ah, a young crest cat. Nearly full grown now, apparently, and . . ."

"Why, yes!" Telzey cried.

The zoologist looked at her. "You knew that . . ."

"Well, not really," Telzey admitted. "Or sort of." She laughed, her cheeks flushed. "This is the most . . . go ahead, please! Sorry I interrupted." She stared at the wall beyond Dr. Droon with a rapt expression.

The zoologist and Halet exchanged glances. Then Dr. Droon resumed cautiously. The crest cats, he said, were a species native to Jontarou. Their existence had been known for only eight years. The species appeared to have had a somewhat limited range—the Baluit Mountains on the opposite side of the huge continent on which Port Nichay had been built. . . .

Telzey barely heard him. A very curious thing was happening. For every sentence Dr. Droon uttered, a dozen other sentences appeared in her awareness. More accurately, it was as if an instantaneous smooth flow of information relevant to whatever he said arose continuously from what might have been almost her own memory, but wasn't. Within a minute or two, she knew more about the crest cats of Jontarou than Dr. Droon could have told her in hours . . . much more than he'd ever known.

She realized suddenly that he'd stopped talking, that he had asked her a question. "Miss Amberdon?" he repeated now, with a note of uncertainty.

"Yar-rrr-REE!" Telzey told him softly. "I'll drink your blood!"

"Eh?"

Telzey blinked, focused on Dr. Droon, wrenching her mind away from a splendid view of the misty-blue peak of the Baluit range. . . .

"Sorry," she said briskly. "Just a joke!" She smiled. "Now what were you saying?"

The zoologist looked at her in a rather odd manner for a moment. "I was inquiring," he said then, "whether you were familiar with the sporting rules established by the various hunting associations of the Hub in connection with the taking of game trophies?"

Telzey shook her head. "No, I never heard of them."

The rules, Dr. Droon explained, laid down the type of equipment—weapons, spotting and tracking instruments, number of assistants, and so forth—a sportsman could legitimately use in the pursuit of any specific type of game. "Before the end of the first year after their discovery," he went on, "the Baluit crest cats had been placed in the ultra-equipment class."

"What's ultra-equipment?" Telzey asked.

"Well," Dr. Droon said thoughtfully, "it doesn't quite involve the use of full battle armor . . . not quite! And, of course, even with that classification the sporting principle of mutual accessibility must be observed."

"Mutual . . . oh, I see!" Telzey paused as another wave of silent information rose into her awareness; went on, "So the game has to be able to get at the sportsman too, eh?"

"That's correct. Except in the pursuit of various classes of flying animals, a shikari would not, for example, be permitted the use of an aircar other than as a means of simple transportation. Under these conditions, it was soon established that crest cats were being obtained by sportsmen who went after them at a rather consistent one-to-one ratio."

Telzey's eyes widened. She'd gathered something similar from her other information source but hadn't quite believed it. "One hunter killed for each cat bagged?" she said. "That's pretty rough sport, isn't it?"

"Extremely rough sport!" Dr. Droon agreed dryly. "In fact, when the statistics were published, the sporting interest in winning a Baluit cat trophy appears to have suffered a sudden and sharp decline. On the other hand, a more scientific interest in these remarkable animals was coincidingly created, and many permits for their acquisition by the agents of museums, universities, public and private collections were issued. Sporting rules, of course, do not apply to that activity. . . ."

Telzey nodded absently. "I see! *They* used aircars, didn't they? A sort of heavy knockout gun—"

"Aircars, long-range detectors and stunguns are standard equipment in such work," Dr. Droon acknowledged. "Gas and poison are employed, of course, as circumstances dictate. The collectors were relatively successful for a while. And then a curious thing happened. Less than two years after their existence became known, the crest cats of the Baluit range were extinct! The inroads made on their numbers by man cannot begin to account for this, so it must be assumed that a sudden plague wiped them out. At any rate, not another living member of the species has been seen on Jontarou until you landed here with your pet last night."

Telzey sat silent for some seconds. Not because of what he had said, but because the other knowledge was still flowing into her mind. On one very important point *that* was at variance with what the zoologist had stated, and from there a coldly logical pattern was building up. Telzey didn't grasp the pattern in complete detail yet, but what she saw of it stirred her with a half-incredulous dread.

She asked, shaping the words carefully, but with only a small part of her attention on what she was really saying, "Just what does all that have to do with Tick-Tock, Dr. Droon?"

Dr. Droon glanced at Halet, and returned his gaze to Telzey. Looking very uncomfortable but quite determined, he told her, "Miss Amberdon, there is a Federation law which states that when a species is threatened with extinction, any available survivors must be transferred to the Life Banks of the University League, to ensure their indefinite preservation. Under the circumstances, this law applies to, ah, Tick-Tock!"

III

So that had been Halet's trick. . . . She'd found out about the crest cats, might have put in as much as a few months arranging to make the discovery of TT's origin on Jontarou seem a regrettable mischance— something no one could have foreseen or prevented. In the Life Banks, from what Telzey had heard of them, TT would cease to exist as an individual awareness while scientists tinkered around with the possibilities of reconstructing her species.

Telzey studied her aunt's carefully sympathizing face for an instant, then asked Dr. Droon, "What about the other crest cats you said were collected before they became extinct here? Wouldn't they be enough for what the Life Banks need?"

He shook his head. "Two immature male specimens are known to exist, and they are at present in the Life Banks. The others that were taken alive at the time have been destroyed . . . often under nearly disastrous circumstances. They are enormously cunning, enormously savage creatures, Miss Amberdon! The additional fact that they can conceal themselves to the point of being virtually undetectable except by the use of instruments makes them one of the most dangerous animals known. Since the young female which you raised as a pet has remained docile, so far, you may not really be able to appreciate that."

"Perhaps I can," Telzey said. She nodded at the heavy-looking instrument standing beside his chair. "And that's . . ."

"It's a life detector combined with a stungun, Miss Amberdon. I have no intention of harming your pet, but we can't take chances with an animal of that type. The gun's charge will knock it unconscious for several minutes—just long enough to let me secure it with paralysis belts."

"You're a collector for the Life Banks, Dr. Droon?"

"That's correct."

"Dr. Droon," Halet remarked, "has obtained a permit from the Planetary Moderator, authorizing him to claim Tick-Tock for the University League and remove her from the planet, dear. So you see there is simply nothing we can do about the matter! Your mother wouldn't like us to attempt to obstruct the law, would she?" Halet paused. "The permit should have your signature, Telzey, but I can sign in your stead if necessary."

That was Halet's way of saying it would do no good to appeal to Jontarou's Planetary Moderator. She'd taken the precaution of getting his assent to the matter first.

"So now if you'll just call Tick-Tock, dear . . ." Halet went on.

Telzey barely heard the last words. She felt herself stiffening slowly, while the living room almost faded from her sight. Perhaps, in that instant, some additional new circuit had closed in her mind, or some additional new channel had opened, for TT's purpose in tricking her into contact with the reckless, mocking beings outside was suddenly and numbingly clear.

And what it meant immediately was that she'd

have to get out of the house without being spotted at it, and go some place where she could be undisturbed for half an hour or more. . . .

She realized that Halet and the zoologist were both staring at her.

"Are you ill, dear?"

"No." Telzey stood up. It would be worse than useless to try to tell these two anything! Her face must be pretty white at the moment—she could feel it—but they assumed, of course, that the shock of losing TT had just now sunk in on her.

"I'll have to check on that law you mentioned before I sign anything," she told Dr. Droon.

"Why, yes . . ." He started to get out of his chair. "I'm sure that can be arranged, Miss Amberdon!"

"Don't bother to call the Moderator's office," Telzey said. "I brought my law library along. I'll look it up myself." She turned to leave the room.

"My niece," Halet explained to Dr. Droon, who was beginning to look puzzled, "attends law school. She's always so absorbed in her studies . . . Telzey?"

"Yes, Halet?" Telzey paused at the door.

"I'm very glad you've decided to be sensible about this, dear. But don't take too long, will you? We don't want to waste Dr. Droon's time."

"It shouldn't take more than five or ten minutes," Telzey told her agreeably. She closed the door behind her, and went directly to her bedroom on the second floor. One of her two valises was still unpacked. She locked the door behind her, opened the unpacked valise, took out a pocket edition law library and sat down at the table with it.

She clicked on the library's viewscreen, tapped the clearing and index buttons. Behind the screen, one of the multiple rows of pinhead tapes shifted slightly as the index was flicked into reading position. Half a minute later, she was glancing over the legal section on which Dr. Droon had based his claim. The library confirmed what he had said.

Very neat of Halet, Telzey thought, very nasty . . . and pretty idiotic! Even a second-year law student could think immediately of two or three ways in which a case like that could have been dragged out in the Federation's courts for a couple of decades before the question of handing Tick-Tock over to the Life Banks became too acute.

Well, Halet simply wasn't really intelligent. And the plot to shanghai TT was hardly even a side issue now. . . .

Telzey snapped the tiny library shut, fastened it to the belt of her sunsuit and went over to the open window. A two-foot ledge passed beneath the window, leading to the roof of a patio on the right. Fifty yards beyond the patio, the garden ended in a natural stone wall. Behind it lay one of the big wooded park areas which formed most of the ground level of Port Nichay.

Tick-Tock wasn't in sight. A sound of voices came from ground-floor windows on the left. Halet had brought her maid and chauffeur along; and a chef had shown up in time to make breakfast this morning, as

part of the city's guest house service. Telzey took the
empty valise to the window, set it on end against the
left side of the frame, and let the window slide down
until its lower edge rested on the valise. She went back
to the house guard-screen panel beside the door, put
her finger against the lock button, and pushed.

The sound of voices from the lower floor was cut off
as outer doors and windows slid silently shut all about
the house. Telzey glanced back at the window. The
valise had creaked a little as the guard field drove the
frame down on it, but it was supporting the thrust. She
returned to the window, wriggled feet foremost
through the opening, twisted around and got a footing
on the ledge.

A minute later, she was scrambling quietly down a
vine-covered patio trellis to the ground. Even after
they discovered she was gone, the guard screen would
keep everybody in the house for some little while.
They'd either have to disengage the screen's main
mechanisms and start poking around in them, or force
open the door to her bedroom and get the lock unset.
Either approach would involve confusion, upset tempers, and generally delay any organized pursuit.

Telzey edged around the patio and started towards
the wall, keeping close to the side of the house so she
couldn't be seen from the windows. The shrubbery
made minor rustling noises as she threaded her way
through it . . . and then there was a different stirring
which might have been no more than a slow, steady

current of air moving among the bushes behind her. She shivered involuntarily but didn't look back.

She came to the wall, stood still, measuring its height, jumped and got an arm across it, swung up a knee and squirmed up and over. She came down on her feet with a small thump in the grass on the other side, glanced back once at the guest house, crossed a path and went on among the park trees.

Within a few hundred yards, it became apparent that she had an escort. She didn't look around for them, but they spread out to the right and left like a skirmish line, keeping abreast with her. Occasional shadows slid silently through patches of open, sunlit ground, disappeared again under the trees. Otherwise, there was hardly anyone in sight. Port Nichay's human residents appeared to make almost no personal use of the vast parkland spread out beneath their tower apartments; and its traffic moved over the airways, visible from the ground only as rainbow-hued ribbons which bisected the sky between the upper tower levels. An occasional private aircar went by overhead.

Wisps of thought which were not her own thoughts flicked through Telzey's mind from moment to moment as the silent line of shadows moved deeper into the park with her. She realized she was being sized up, judged, evaluated again. No more information was coming through; they had given her as much information as she needed. In the main perhaps, they were simply curious now. This was the first human mind they'd been able to make heads or tails of which hadn't seemed deaf and silent to their form of communication. They were taking time out to study it. They'd been assured she would have something of genuine importance to tell them; and there was some derision about that. But they were willing to wait a little, and find out. They were curious and they liked games. At the moment, Telzey, and what she might try to do to change their plans, was the game on which their attention was fixed.

Twelve minutes passed before the talker on Telzey's wrist began to buzz. It continued to signal off and on for another few minutes, then stopped. Back in the guest house they couldn't be sure yet whether she wasn't simply locked inside her room and refusing to answer them. But Telzey quickened her pace.

The park's trees gradually became more massive, reached higher above her, stood paced more widely apart. She passed through the morning shadow of the residential tower nearest the guest house, and emerged from it presently on the shore of a small lake. On the other side of the lake, a number of dappled grazing animals like long-necked, tall horses lifted their heads to watch her. For some seconds they seemed only mildly interested, but then a breeze moved across the lake, crinkling the surface of the water; and as it touched the opposite shore, abrupt panic exploded among the grazers. They wheeled, went flashing away in effortless twenty-foot strides, and were gone among the trees.

Telzey felt a crawling along her spine. It was the first objective indication she'd had of the nature of the company she had brought to the lake, and while it hardly came as a surprise, for a moment her urge was to follow the example of the grazers.

"Tick-Tock?" she whispered, suddenly a little short of breath.

A single up-and-down purring note replied from the bushes on her right. TT was still around, for whatever good that might do. Not too much, Telzey thought, if it came to serious trouble. But the knowledge was somewhat reassuring . . . and this, meanwhile, appeared to be as far as she needed to get from the guest house. They'd be looking for her by aircar presently, but there was nothing to tell them in which direction to turn first.

She climbed the bank of the lake to a point where she was screened both by thick, green shrubbery and the top of a single immense tree from the sky, sat down on some dry, mossy growth, took the law library from her belt, opened it and placed it in her lap. Vague stirrings indicated that her escort was also settling down in an irregular circle about her; and apprehension shivered on Telzey's skin again. It wasn't that their attitude was hostile; they were simply overawing. And no one could predict what they might do next. Without looking up, she asked a question in her mind.

"Ready?"

Sense of multiple acknowledgment, variously tinged —sardonic, interestedly amused, attentive, doubtful. Impatience quivered through it too, only tentatively held in restraint, and Telzey's forehead was suddenly wet. Some of them seemed on the verge of expressing disapproval with what was being done here.

Her fingers quickly flicked in the index tape, and the stir of feeling about her subsided, their attention captured again for the moment. Her thoughts became to some degree detached, ready to dissect another problem in the familiar ways and present the answers to it. Not a very involved problem essentially, but this time it wasn't a school exercise. Her company waited, withdrawn, silent, aloof once more, while the index blurred, checked, blurred and checked. Within a minute and a half, she had noted a dozen reference symbols. She tapped in another of the pinhead tapes, glanced over a few paragraphs, licked salty sweat from her lip, and said in her thoughts, emphasizing the meaning of each detail of the sentence so that there would be no misunderstanding, "This is the Federation law that applies to the situation which existed originally on this planet. . . ."

There were no interruptions, no commenting thoughts, no intrusions of any kind, as she went step by step through the section, turned to another one, and another. In perhaps twelve minutes she came to the end of the last one, and stopped. Instantly, argument exploded about her.

Telzey was not involved in the argument; in fact,

she could grasp only scraps of it. Either they were excluding her deliberately, or the exchange was too swift, practiced and varied to allow her to keep up. But their vehemence was not encouraging. And was it reasonable to assume that the Federation's laws would have any meaning for minds like these? Telzey snapped the library shut with fingers that had begun to tremble, and placed it on the ground. Then she stiffened. In the sensations washing about her, a special excitement rose suddenly, a surge of almost gleeful wildness that choked away her breath. Awareness followed of a pair of malignant crimson eyes fastened on her, moving steadily closer. A kind of nightmare paralysis seized Telzey—they'd turned her over to that red-eyed horror! She sat still, feeling mouse-sized.

Something came out with a crash from a thicket behind her. Her muscles went tight. But it was TT who rubbed a hard head against her shoulder, took another three stiff-legged steps forward and stopped between Telzey and the bushes on their right, back rigid, neck fur erect, tail twisting.

Expectant silence closed in about them. The circle was waiting. In the greenery on the right something made a slow, heavy stir.

TT's lips peeled back from her teeth. Her head swung towards the motion, ears flattening, transformed to a split, snarling demon-mask. A long shriek ripped from her lungs, raw with fury, blood lust and challenge.

The sound died away. For some seconds the tension

about them held; then came a sense of gradual relaxation mingled with a partly amused approval. Telzey was shaking violently. It had been, she was telling herself, a deliberate test . . . . not of herself, of course, but of TT. And Tick-Tock had passed with honors. That *her* nerves had been half ruined in the process would seem a matter of no consequence to this rugged crew. . . .

She realized next that someone here was addressing her personally.

It took a few moments to steady her jittering thoughts enough to gain a more definite impression than that. This speaker, she discovered then, was a member of the circle of whom she hadn't been aware before. The thought-impressions came hard and cold as iron—it was a personage who was very evidently in the habit of making major decisions and seeing them carried out. The circle, its moment of sport over, was listening with more than a suggestion of deference. Tick-Tock, far from conciliated, green eyes still blazing, nevertheless was settling down to listen too.

Telzey began to understand.

Her suggestions, Iron Thoughts informed her, might appear without value to a number of foolish minds here, but *he* intended to see they were given a fair trial. Did he perhaps hear, he inquired next of the circle, throwing in a casual but horridly vivid impression of snapping spines and slashed shaggy throats spouting blood, any objection to that?

Dead stillness all around. There was, definitely, no

objection! Tick-Tock began to grin like a pleased kitten.

That point having been settled in an orderly manner now, Iron Thoughts went on coldly to Telzey: what specifically did she propose they should do?

IV

Halet's long, pearl-gray sportscar showed up above the park trees twenty minutes later. Telzey, face turned down towards the open law library in her lap, watched the car from the corner of her eyes. She was in plain view, sitting beside the lake, apparently absorbed in legal research. Tick-Tock, camouflaged among the bushes thirty feet higher up the bank, had spotted the car an instant before she did and announced the fact with a three-second break in her purring. Neither of them made any other move.

The car was approaching the lake but still a good distance off. Its canopy was down, and Telzey could just make out the heads of three people inside. Delquos, Halet's chauffeur, would be flying the vehicle, while Halet and Dr. Droon looked around for her from the sides. Three hundred yards away, the aircar began a turn to the right. Delquos didn't like his employer much; at a guess, he had just spotted Telzey and was trying to warn her off.

Telzey closed the library and put it down, picked up a handful of pebbles and began flicking them idly, one at a time, into the water. The aircar vanished to her left.

Three minutes later, she watched its shadow glide across the surface of the lake towards her. Her heart began to thump almost audibly, but she didn't look up. Tick-Tock's purring continued, on its regular, unhurried note. The car came to a stop almost directly overhead. After a couple of seconds, there was a clicking noise. The purring ended abruptly.

Telzey climbed to her feet as Delquos brought the car down to the bank of the lake. The chauffeur grinned ruefully at her. A side door had been opened, and Halet and Dr. Droon stood behind it. Halet watched Telzey with a small smile while the naturalist put the heavy life-detector-and-stungun device carefully down on the floorboards.

"If you're looking for Tick-Tock," Telzey said, "she isn't here."

Halet shook her head sorrowfully.

"There's no use lying to us, dear! Dr. Droon just stunned her."

They found TT collapsed on her side among the shrubs, wearing her natural color. Her eyes were shut; her chest rose and fell in a slow breathing motion. Dr. Droon, looking rather apologetic, pointed out to Telzey that her pet was in no pain, that the stungun had simply put her comfortably to sleep. He also explained the use of the two sets of webbed paralysis belts which he fastened about TT's legs. The effect of the stun charge would wear off in a few minutes, and contact with the inner surfaces of the energized belts would then keep TT anesthetized and unable to move until the belts were removed. She would, he repeated, be suffering no pain through the process.

Telzey didn't comment. She watched Delquos raise TT's limp body above the level of the bushes with a gravity hoist belonging to Dr. Droon, and maneuver her back to the car, the others following. Delquos climbed into the car first, opened the big trunk compartment in the rear. TT was slid inside and the trunk compartment locked.

"Where are you taking her?" Telzey asked sullenly as Delquos lifted the car into the air.

"To the spaceport, dear," Halet said. "Dr. Droon and I both felt it would be better to spare your feelings by not prolonging the matter unnecessarily."

Telzey wrinkled her nose disdainfully, and walked up the aircar to stand behind Delquos's seat. She leaned against the back of the seat for an instant. Her legs felt shaky.

The chauffer gave her a sober wink from the side.

"That's a dirty trick she's played on you, Miss Telzey!" he murmured. "I tried to warn you."

"I know." Telzey took a deep breath. "Look, Delquos, in just a minute something's going to happen! It'll look dangerous, but it won't be. Don't let it get you nervous . . . right?"

"Huh?" Delquos appeared startled, but kept his voice low. "Just *what's* going to happen?"

"No time to tell you. Remember what I said."

Telzey moved back a few steps from the driver's seat, turned around, said unsteadily, "Halet, Dr. Droon . . ."

Halet had been speaking quietly to Dr. Droon; they both looked up.

"If you don't move, and don't do anything stupid," Telzey said rapidly, "you won't get hurt. If you do . . . well, I don't know! You see, there's another crest cat in the car . . ." In her mind she added, "Now!"

It was impossible to tell in just what section of the car Iron Thoughts had been lurking. The carpeting near the rear passenger seats seemed to blur for an instant. Then he was there, camouflage dropped, sitting on the floorboards five feet from the naturalist and Halet.

Halet's mouth opened wide; she tried to scream but fainted instead. Dr. Droon's right hand started out quickly towards the big stungun device beside his seat. Then he checked himself and sat still, ashen-faced.

Telzey didn't blame him for changing his mind. She felt he must be a remarkably brave man to have moved at all. Iron Thoughts, twice as broad across the back as Tick-Tock, twice as massively muscled, looked like a devil-beast even to her. His dark-green marbled hide was criss-crossed with old scar patterns; half his tossing crimson crest appeared to have been ripped away. He reached out now in a fluid, silent motion, hooked a paw under the stungun and flicked upwards. The big instrument rose in an incredibly swift, steep arc eighty feet into the air, various parts flying away from it, before it started curving down towards the treetops below the car. Iron Thoughts lazily swung his head around and looked at Telzey with yellow fire-eyes.

"Miss Telzey! Miss Telzey!" Delquos was muttering behind her. "You're *sure* it won't . . ."

Telzey swallowed. At the moment, she felt barely mouse-sized again. "Just relax!" she told Delquos in a shaky voice. "He's really quite t-t-t-tame."

Iron Thoughts produced a harsh but not unamiable chuckle in her mind.

The pearl-gray sportscar, covered now by its streamlining canopy, drifted down presently to a parking platform outside the suite of offices of Jontarou's Planetary Moderator, on the fourteenth floor of the Shikaris' Club Tower. An attendant waved it on into a vacant slot.

Inside the car, Delquos set the brakes, switched off the engine, asked, "Now what?"

"I think," Telzey said reflectively, "we'd better lock you in the trunk compartment with my aunt and Dr. Droon while I talk to the Moderator."

The chauffeur shrugged. He'd regained most of his aplomb during the unhurried trip across the parklands. Iron Thoughts had done nothing but sit in the center of the car, eyes half shut, looking like instant death, enjoying a dignified nap and occasionally emitting a ripsawing noise which might have been either his style of purring or a snore. And Tick-Tock, when Delquos peeled the paralysis belts off her legs at Telzey's direction, had greeted him with her usual reserved affability. What the chauffeur was suffering from at the moment was mainly intense curiosity, which Telzey had done nothing to relieve.

"Just as you say, Miss Telzey," he agreed. "I hate to miss whatever you're going to be doing here, but if you *don't* lock me up now, Miss Halet will figure I was helping you and fire me as soon as you let her out."

Telzey nodded, then cocked her head in the direction of the rear compartment. Faint sounds coming through the door indicated that Halet had regained consciousness and was having hysterics.

"You might tell her," Telzey suggested, "that there'll be a grown-up crest cat sitting outside the compartment door." This wasn't true, but neither Delquos nor Halet could know it. "If there's too much racket before I get back, it's likely to irritate him. . . ."

A minute later, she set both car doors on lock and went outside, wishing she was less informally clothed. Sunbriefs and sandals tended to make her look juvenile.

The parking attendant appeared startled when she approached him with Tick-Tock striding along beside her.

"They'll never let you into the offices with that thing, miss," he informed her. "Why, it doesn't even have a collar!"

"Don't worry about it," Telzey told him aloofly. She dropped a two-credit piece she'd taken from Halet's purse into his hand, and continued on towards the building entrance. The attendant squinted after her, trying unsuccessfully to dispel an odd impression that the big catlike animal with the girl was throwing a double shadow.

The Moderator's chief receptionist also had some doubts about TT, and possibly about the sunbriefs, though she seemed impressed when Telzey's identification tag informed her she was speaking to the daughter of Federation Councilwoman Jessamine Amberdon.

"You feel you can discuss this—emergency—only with the Moderator himself, Miss Amberdon?" she repeated.

"Exactly," Telzey said firmly. A buzzer sounded as she spoke. The receptionist excused herself and picked up an earphone. She listened a moment, said blandly, "Yes. Of course. Yes, I understand," replaced the earphone and stood up, smiling at Telzey.

"Would you come with me, Miss Amberdon?" she said. "I think the Moderator will see you immediately."

Telzey followed her, chewing thoughtfully at her lip. This was easier than she'd expected—in fact, too easy! Halet's work? Probably. A few comments to the effect of "a highly imaginative child . . . overexcitable," while Halet was arranging to have the Moderator's office authorize Tick-Tock's transfer to the Life Banks, along with the implication that Jessamine Amberdon would appreciate a discreet handling of any disturbance Telzey might create as a result.

It was the sort of notion that would appeal to Halet. . . .

They passed through a series of elegantly equipped offices and hallways, Telzey grasping TT's neck-fur in lieu of a leash, their appearance creating a tactfully restrained wave of surprise among secretaries and clerks. And if somebody here and there was troubled by a fleeting, uncanny impression that not one large beast but two seemed to be trailing the Moderator's visitor down the aisles, no mention was made of what could have been only a momentary visual distortion. Finally, a pair of sliding doors opened ahead, and the receptionist ushered Telzey into a large, cool balcony garden on the shaded side of the great building. A tall, gray-haired man stood up from the desk at which he was working, and bowed to Telzey. The receptionist withdrew again.

"My pleasure, Miss Amberdon," Jontarou's Planetary Moderator said. "Be seated, please." He studied Tick-Tock with more than casual interest while Telzey was settling herself into a chair, added, "And what may I and my office do for you?"

Telzey hesitated. She'd observed his type on Orado in her mother's circle of acquaintances . . . a senior diplomat, a man not easy to impress. It was a safe bet that he'd had her brought out to his balcony office only to keep her occupied while Halet was quietly informed where the Amberdon problem child was and requested to come over and take charge.

What she had to tell him now would have sounded rather wild even if presented by a presumably responsible adult. She could provide proof, but until the Moderator was already nearly sold on her story, that would be a very unsafe thing to do. Old Iron Thoughts was backing her up, but if it didn't look as if her plans were likely to succeed, he would be willing to ride herd on his devil's pack just so long. . . .

Better start the ball rolling without any preliminaries, Telzey decided. The Moderator's picture of her must be that of a spoiled, neurotic brat in a stew about the threatened loss of a pet animal. He expected her to start arguing with him immediately about Tick-Tock.

She said, "Do you have a personal interest in keeping the Baluit crest cats from becoming extinct?"

Surprise flickered in his eyes for an instant. Then he smiled.

"I admit I do, Miss Amberdon," he said pleasantly. "I should like to see the species re-established. I count myself almost uniquely fortunate in having had the opportunity to bag two of the magnificent brutes before disease wiped them out on the planet."

The last seemed a less than fortunate statement just now. Telzey felt a sharp tingle of alarm, then sensed that in the minds which were drawing the meaning of the Moderator's speech from her mind there had been only a brief stir of interest.

She cleared her throat, said, "The point is that they weren't wiped out by disease."

He considered quizzically, seemed to wonder what she was trying to lead up to. Telzey gathered her courage, plunged on, "Would you like to hear what did happen?"

"I should be much interested, Miss Amberdon," the Moderator said without change of expression. "But first, if you'll excuse me a moment . . ."

There had been some signal from his desk which

Telzey hadn't noticed, because he picked up a small communicator now, said, "Yes?" After a few seconds, he resumed, "That's rather curious, isn't it? Yes, I'd try that. No, that shouldn't be necessary. . . . Yes, please do. Thank you." He replaced the communicator, his face very sober; then, his eyes flicking for an instant to TT, he drew one of the upper desk drawers open a few inches, and turned back to Telzey.

"Now, Miss Amberdon," he said affably, "you were about to say? About these crest cats . . ."

Telzey swallowed. She hadn't heard the other side of the conversation, but she could guess what it had been about. His office had called the guest house, had been told by Halet's maid that Halet, the chauffeur and Dr. Droon were out looking for Miss Telzey and her pet. The Moderator's office had then checked on the sports-car's communication number and attempted to call it. And, of course, there had been no response.

To the Moderator, considering what Halet would have told him, it must add up to the grim possibility that the young lunatic he was talking to had let her three-quarters-grown crest cat slaughter her aunt and the two men when they caught up with her! The office would be notifying the police now to conduct an immediate search for the missing aircar.

When it would occur to them to look for it on the Moderator's parking terrace was something Telzey couldn't know. But if Halet and Dr. Droon were released before the Moderator accepted her own version of what had occurred, and the two reported the presence of wild crest cats in Port Nichay, there would be almost no possibility of keeping the situation under control. Somebody was bound to make some idiotic move, and the fat would be in the fire. . . .

Two things might be in her favor. The Moderator seemed to have the sort of steady nerve one would expect in a man who had bagged two Baluit crest cats. The partly opened desk drawer beside him must have a gun in it; apparently he considered that a sufficient precaution against an attack by TT. He wasn't likely to react in a panicky manner. And the mere fact that he suspected Telzey of homicidal tendencies would make him give the closest attention to what she said. Whether he believed her then was another matter, of course.

Slightly encouraged, Telzey began to talk. It did sound like a thoroughly wild story, but the Moderator listened with an appearance of intent interest. When she had told him as much as she felt he could be expected to swallow for a start, he said musingly, "So they weren't wiped out—they went into hiding! Do I understand you to say they did it to avoid being hunted?"

Telzey chewed her lip frowningly before replying. "There's something about that part I don't quite get," she admitted. "Of course I don't quite get either why you'd want to go hunting . . . twice for something that's just as likely to bag you instead!"

"Well, those are, ah, merely the statistical odds," the Moderator explained. "If one has enough confidence, you see . . ."

"I don't really. But the crest cats seem to have felt

the same way—at first. They were getting around one hunter for every cat that got shot. Humans were the most exciting game they'd ever run into.

"But then that ended, and the humans started knocking them out with stunguns from aircars where they couldn't be got at, and hauling them off while they were helpless. After it had gone on for a while, they decided to keep out of sight.

"But they're still around . . . thousands and thousands of them! Another thing nobody's known about them is that they weren't only in the Baluit Mountains. There were crest cats scattered all through the big forests along the other side of the continent."

"Very interesting," the Moderator commented. "Very interesting, indeed!" He glanced towards the communicator, then returned his gaze to Telzey, drumming his fingers lightly on the desk top.

She could tell nothing at all from his expression now, but she guessed he was thinking hard. There was supposed to be no native intelligent life in the legal sense on Jontarou, and she had been careful to say nothing so far to make the Baluit cats look like more than rather exceptionally intelligent animals. The next —rather large—question should be how she'd come by such information.

If the Moderator asked her that, Telzey thought, she could feel she'd made a beginning at getting him to buy the whole story. . . .

"Well," he said abruptly, "if the crest cats are not

extinct or threatened with extinction, the Life Banks obviously have no claim on your pet." He smiled confidingly at her. "And that's the reason you're here, isn't it?"

"Well, no," Telzey began, dismayed. "I . . ."

"Oh, it's quite all right, Miss Amberdon! I'll simply rescind the permit which was issued for the purpose. You need feel no further concern about that." He paused. "Now, just one question . . . do you happen to know where your aunt is at present?"

Telzey had a dead, sinking feeling. So he hadn't believed a word she said. He'd been stalling her along until the aircar could be found.

She took a deep breath. "You'd better listen to the rest of it."

"Why, is there more?" the Moderator asked politely.

"Yes. The important part! The kind of creatures they are, they couldn't go into hiding indefinitely just because someone was after them."

Was there a flicker of something beyond watchfulness in his expression? "What would they do, Miss Amberdon?" he asked quietly.

"If they couldn't get at the men in the aircars and couldn't communicate with them"—the flicker again!—"they'd start looking for the place the men came from, wouldn't they? It might take them some years to work their way across the continent and locate us here in Port Nichay. But supposing they did it finally and a few thousand of them were sitting around in the parks

down there right now? They could come up the side of
these towers as easily as they go up the side of a mountain. And supposing they'd decided that the only way to
handle the problem was to clean out the human beings in Port Nichay?"

The Moderator stared at her in silence a few seconds. "You're saying," he observed then, "that they're
rational beings—above the Critical I.Q. level."

"Well," Telzey said, "legally they're rational. I
checked on that. About as rational as we are, I
suppose."

"And would you mind telling me now how you happen to know these things?"

"They told me," Telzey said bluntly.

He was silent again, studying her face. "You mentioned, Miss Amberdon, that they have been unable to
communicate with other human beings. This suggests
then that you are a xenotelepath. . . ."

"I am?" Telzey hadn't heard the term before. "If it
means that I can tell what the cats are thinking, and
they can tell what I'm thinking, I guess that's the word
for it." She considered him, decided she had him almost on the ropes, went on quickly, "I looked up the
laws, and told them they could conclude a treaty with
the Federation which would establish them as an Affiliated Species . . . and that would settle everything the
way they would want it settled, without trouble. Some
of them believed me. They decided to wait until I could
talk to you. If it works out, fine! If it doesn't"—she

felt her voice falter for an instant—"they're going to cut loose fast!"

The Moderator seemed undisturbed. "And what am I supposed to do?"

"I told them you'd contact the Council of the Federation on Orado."

"Contact the Council?" he repeated coolly. "With no more proof for this story than your word, Miss Amberdon?"

Telzey felt a quick, angry stirring begin about her, felt her face whiten.

"All right," she said. "I'll give you proof! I'll have to now. But that'll be it. Once they've tipped their hand all the way, you'll have about thirty seconds left to make the right move. I hope you remember that!"

He cleared his throat. "I . . ."

"NOW!" Telzey said.

Along the walls of the balcony garden, beside the ornamental flower stands, against the edges of the rock pool, the crest cats appeared. Perhaps thirty of them. None quite as physically impressive as Iron Thoughts, who stood closest to the Moderator, but none very far from it. Motionless as rocks, frightening as gargoyles, they waited, eyes glowing with hellish excitement.

"This is *their* council, you see," Telzey heard herself saying. "The chiefs of the tribes . . '

The Moderator's face had also paled. But he was, after all, an old shikari and a senior diplomat. He took an unhurried look around the circle, said quietly, "Accept my profound apologies for doubting you, Miss Amberdon!" and reached for the desk communicator.

Iron Thoughts swung his demon head in Telzey's direction. For an instant, she picked up the mental impression of a fierce yellow eye closing in an approving wink.

". . . an open transmitter line to Orado," the Moderator was saying into the communicator. "The Council. And snap it up! Some very important visitors are waiting. . . ."

The offices of Jontarou's Planetary Moderator became an extremely busy and interesting area then. Quite two hours passed before it occurred to anyone to ask Telzey again whether she knew where her aunt was at present.

Telzey smote her forehead.

"Forgot all about that!" she admitted, fishing the sportscar's keys out of the pocket of her sunbriefs. "They're out on the parking platform. . . ."

When the trunk compartment was opened, Delquos and Dr. Droon looked rather worn out. Halet was still having hysterics.

V

The preliminary treaty arrangements between the Federation of the Hub and the new Affiliated Species of the Planet of Jontarou were formally ratified two weeks later, the ceremony taking place on Jontarou, in the Champagne Hall of the Shikaris' Club.

Telzey was able to follow the event only by news viewer in her ship-cabin, she and Halet being on the return trip to Orado by then. She wasn't too interested in the treaty's details—they conformed almost exactly to what she had read out to Iron Thoughts and his co-chiefs and companions in the park. It was the smooth bridging of the wide language gap between the contracting parties by a row of interpreting machines and a handful of human xenotelepaths which held her attention.

As she switched off the viewer, Halet came wandering in from the adjoining cabin.

"I was watching it too!" Halet observed. She smiled. "I was hoping to see dear Tick-Tock."

Telzey looked over at her. "Well, TT would hardly be likely to show up in Port Nichay," she said. "She's having too good a time now finding out what life in the Baluit range is like."

"I suppose so," Halet agreed doubtfully, sitting down on a hassock. "But I'm glad she promised to get in touch with us again in a few years. I'll miss her."

Telzey regarded her aunt with a reflective frown. Halet meant it quite sincerely, of course; she had undergone a profound change of heart during the past two weeks. But Telzey wasn't without some doubts about the actual value of a change of heart brought on by telepathic means. The learning process the crest cats had started in her mind appeared to have con-

tinued automatically several days longer than her
rugged teachers had really intended; and Telzey had
reason to believe that by the end of that time she'd developed associated latent abilities of which the crest
cats had never heard. She'd barely begun to get it all
sorted out yet, but, as an example, she'd found it remarkably easy to turn Halet's more obnoxious attitudes virtually upside down. It had taken her a
couple of days to get the hang of her aunt's personal
symbolism, but after that there had been no problem.
The question remained whether it had been such a
good thing to do.

She was reasonably certain she'd broken no laws so
far, though the sections in the law library covering the
use and abuse of psionic abilities were veiled in such
intricate and downright obscuring phrasing—deliberately, Telzey suspected—that it was really difficult
to say what they did mean. But even aside from that,
there were a number of arguments in favor of exer-
cising great caution.

Jessamine, for one thing, was bound to start worrying about her sister-in-law's health if Halet turned up
on Orado in her present state of mind, even though it
would make for a far more agreeable atmosphere in
the Amberdon household. . . .

"Halet," Telzey inquired mentally, "do you remember what an all-out stinker you used to be?"

"Of course, dear," Halet said aloud. "I can hardly
wait to tell dear Jessamine how much I regret the
many times I—"

"Well," Telzey went on, still verbalizing it silently, "I think you'd really enjoy life more if you were, let's say, about halfway between your old nasty self and the sort of sickening-good kind you are now."

"Why, Telzey!" Halet cried out with dopey amiability. "What a delightful idea!"

"Let's try it," Telzey said.

There was silence in the cabin for some twenty minutes then while she went painstakingly about remolding a number of Halet's character traits for the second time. She still felt some misgiving about it; but if it became necessary, she probably could always restore the old Halet *in toto.*

These, she told herself, definitely were powers one should treat with respect! Better rattle through law school first; then, with that out of the way, she could start hunting around to see who in the Federation was qualified to instruct a genius-level novice in the proper handling of psionics. . . .

Liar!

BY ISAAC ASIMOV

*Of all Isaac Asimov's many contributions
to the body of ideas making up modern science
fiction, I think his Three Laws of Robotics are
the most significant, since they define the role
of the robot in a way that surely must be
adopted when mechanical men at last go into
factory production. Asimov's Three Laws are:*

*One: A robot may not injure a human being,
or, through inaction, allow a human being to
come to harm.*

*Two: A robot must obey the orders given
it by human beings except where such orders
would conflict with the First Law.*

*Three: A robot must protect its own exis-
tence as long as such protection does not conflict with the First or Second Law.*

*Very logical. But how do you define "injury"?
A robot need not strike a human being to
injure him. What about the subtler sort of
damage a mind-reading robot might do?*

102

*A*lfred *Lanning* lit his cigar carefully, but the tips of his fingers were trembling slightly. His gray eyebrows hunched low as he spoke between puffs.

"It reads minds all right—damn little doubt about that! But why?" He looked at mathematician Peter Bogert. "Well?"

Bogert flattened his black hair down with both hands. "That was the thirty-fourth RB model we've turned out, Lanning. All the others were strictly orthodox."

The third man at the table frowned. Milton Ashe was the youngest officer of U. S. Robot & Mechanical Men, Inc., and proud of his post.

"Listen, Bogert. There wasn't a hitch in the assembly from start to finish. I guarantee that."

Bogert's thick lips spread in a patronizing smile. "Do you? If you can answer for the entire assembly line, I recommend your promotion. By exact count, there are seventy-five thousand, two hundred and thirty-four operations necessary for the manufacture of a single positronic brain, each separate operation depending for successful completion upon any number of factors, from five to a hundred and five. If any one of them goes seriously wrong, the 'brain' is ruined. I quote our own information folder, Ashe."

Milton Ashe flushed, but a fourth voice cut off his reply.

"If we're going to start by trying to fix the blame on

one another, I'm leaving." Susan Calvin's hands were folded tightly in her lap, and the little lines about her thin, pale lips deepened. "We've got a mind-reading robot on our hands and it strikes me as rather important that we find out just why it reads minds. We're not going to do that by saying, 'Your fault! My fault!'"

Her cold gray eyes fastened upon Ashe, and he grinned.

Lanning grinned too, and, as always at such times, his long white hair and shrewd little eyes made him the picture of a biblical patriarch. "True for you, Dr. Calvin."

His voice became suddenly crisp. "Here's everything in pill-concentrate form. We've produced a positronic brain of supposedly ordinary vintage that's got the remarkable property of being able to tune in on thought waves. It would mark the most important advance in robotics in decades, if we knew how it happened. We don't, and we have to find out. Is that clear?"

"May I make a suggestion?" asked Bogert.

"Go ahead!"

"I'd say that until we do figure out the mess—and as a mathematician I expect it to be a very devil of a mess—we keep the existence of RB-34 a secret. I mean even from the other members of the staff. As heads of the departments, we ought not to find it an insoluble problem, and the fewer know about it—"

"Bogert is right," said Dr. Calvin. "Ever since the Interplanetary Code was modified to allow robot models to be tested in the plants before being shipped out to space, antirobot propaganda has increased. If any word leaks out about a robot being able to read minds before we can announce complete control of the phenomenon, pretty effective capital could be made out of it."

Lanning sucked at his cigar and nodded gravely. He turned to Ashe. "I think you said you were alone when you first stumbled on this thought-reading business."

"I'll say I was alone—I got the scare of my life. RB-34 had just been taken off the assembly table and they sent him down to me. Obermann was off somewheres, so I took him down to the testing rooms myself—at least I started to take him down." Ashe paused, and a tiny smile tugged at his lips. "Say, did any of you ever carry on a thought conversation without knowing it?"

No one bothered to answer, and he continued, "You don't realize it at first, you know. He just spoke to me— as logically and sensibly as you can imagine—and it was only when I was most of the way down to the testing rooms that I realized that I hadn't said anything. Sure, I thought lots, but that isn't the same thing, is it? I locked that thing up and ran for Lanning. Having it walking beside me, calmly peering into my thoughts and picking and choosing among them gave me the willies."

"I imagine it would," said Susan Calvin thoughtfully. Her eyes fixed themselves upon Ashe in an oddly intent manner. "We are so accustomed to considering our own thoughts private."

Lanning broke in impatiently, "Then only the four of us know. All right! We've got to go about this systematically. Ashe, I want you to check over the assembly line from beginning to end—everything. You're to eliminate all operations in which there was no possible chance of an error, and list all those where there were, together with its nature and possible magnitude."

"Tall order," grunted Ashe.

"Naturally! Of course, you're to put the men under you to work on this—every single one if you have to, and I don't care if we go behind schedule, either. But they're not to know why, you understand."

"Hm-m-m, yes!" The young technician grinned wryly. "It's still a lulu of a job."

Lanning swiveled about in his chair and faced Calvin. "You'll have to tackle the job from the other direction. You're the robopsychologist of the plant, so you're to study the robot itself and work backward. Try to find out how he ticks. See what else is tied up with his telepathic powers, how far they extend, how they warp his outlook, and just exactly what harm it has done to his ordinary RB properties. You've got that?"

Lanning didn't wait for Dr. Calvin to answer.

"I'll co-ordinate the work and interpret the findings mathematically." He puffed violently at his cigar and mumbled the rest through the smoke, "Bogert will help me there, of course."

Bogert polished the nails of one pudgy hand with the other and said blandly, "I dare say. I know a little in the line."

"Well! I'll get started." Ashe shoved his chair back and rose. His pleasantly youthful face crinkled in a grin. "I've got the darnedest job of any of us, so I'm getting out of here and to work."

He left with a slurred, "B' seein' ye!"

Susan Calvin answered with a barely perceptible nod, but her eyes followed him out of sight and she did not answer when Lanning grunted and said, "Do you want to go up and see RB-34 now, Dr. Calvin?"

RB-34's photoelectric eyes lifted from the book at the muffled sound of hinges turning and he was upon his feet when Susan Calvin entered.

She paused to readjust the huge "No Entrance" sign upon the door and then approached the robot.

"I've brought you the texts upon hyperatomic motors, Herbie—a few anyway. Would you care to look at them?"

RB-34—otherwise known as Herbie—lifted the three heavy books from her arms and opened to the title page of one.

"Hm-m-m! 'Theory of Hyperatomics.' " He mumbled inarticulately to himself as he flipped the pages and then spoke with an abstracted air, "Sit down, Dr. Calvin! This will take me a few minutes."

The psychologist seated herself and watched Herbie narrowly as he took a chair at the other side of the table and went through the three books systematically.

At the end of half an hour, he put them down, "Of course, I know why you brought these."

The corner of Dr. Calvin's lip twitched. "I was afraid you would. It's difficult to work with you, Herbie. You're always a step ahead of me."

"It's the same with these books, you know, as with the others. They just don't interest me. There's nothing to your textbooks. Your science is just a mass of collected data plastered together by makeshift theory —and all so incredibly simple that it's scarcely worth bothering about.

"It's your fiction that interests me. Your studies of the interplay of human motives and emotions"—his mighty hand gestured vaguely as he sought the proper words.

Dr. Calvin whispered, "I think I understand."

"I see into minds, you see," the robot continued, "and you have no idea how complicated they are. I can't begin to understand everything because my own mind has so little in common with them—but I try, and your novels help."

"Yes, but I'm afraid that after going through some of the harrowing emotional experiences of our present-day sentimental novel"—there was a tinge of bitterness in her voice—"you find real minds like ours dull and colorless."

"But I don't!"

The sudden energy in the response brought the other to her feet. She felt herself reddening, and thought wildly, "He must know!"

Herbie subsided suddenly, and muttered in a low voice from which the metallic timbre had departed almost entirely. "But, of course, I know about it, Dr. Calvin. You think of it always, so how can I help but know?"

Her face was hard. "Have you—told anyone?"

"Of course not!" This, with genuine surprise. "No one has asked me."

"Well, then," she flung out, "I suppose you think I am a fool."

"No! It is a normal emotion."

"Perhaps that is why it is so foolish." The wistfulness in her voice drowned out everything else. Some of the woman peered through the layer of doctorhood. "I am not what you would call—attractive."

"If you are referring to mere physical attraction, I couldn't judge. But I know, in any case, that there are other types of attraction."

"Nor young." Dr. Calvin had scarcely heard the robot.

"You are not yet forty." An anxious insistence had crept into Herbie's voice.

"Thirty-eight as you count the years; a shriveled sixty as far as my emotional outlook on life is concerned. Am I a psychologist for nothing?"

She drove on with bitter breathlessness. "And he's barely thirty-five and looks and acts younger. Do you suppose he ever sees me as anything but . . . but what I am?"

"You are wrong!" Herbie's steel fist struck the plastic-topped table with a strident clang. "Listen to me—"

But Susan Calvin whirled on him now and the hunted pain in her eyes became a blaze. "Why should I? What do you know about it all, anyway, you . . . you machine. I'm just a specimen to you; an interesting bug with a peculiar mind spread-eagled for inspection. It's a wonderful example of frustration, isn't it? Almost as good as your books." Her voice, emerging in dry sobs, choked into silence.

The robot cowered at the outburst. He shook his head pleadingly. "Won't you listen to me, please? I could help you if you would let me."

"How?" Her lips curled. "By giving me good advice?"

"No, not that. It's just that I know what other people think—Milton Ashe, for instance."

There was a long silence, and Susan Calvin's eyes dropped. "I don't want to know what he thinks," she gasped. "Keep quiet."

"I think you would want to know what he thinks."

Her head remained bent, but her breath came more quickly. "You are talking nonsense," she whispered.

"Why should I? I am trying to help. Milton Ashe's thoughts of you—" he paused.

And then the psychologist raised her head. "Well?"

The robot said quietly, "He loves you."

For a full minute, Dr. Calvin did not speak. She merely stared. Then, "You are mistaken! You must be. Why should he?"

"But he does. A thing like that cannot be hidden, not from me."

"But I am so . . . so—" she stammered to a halt.

"He looks deeper than the skin, and admires intellect in others. Milton Ashe is not the type to marry a head of hair and a pair of eyes."

Susan Calvin found herself blinking rapidly and waited before speaking. Even then her voice trembled. "Yet he certainly never in any way indicated—"

"Have you ever given him a chance?"

"How could I? I never thought that—"

"Exactly!"

The psychologist paused in thought and then looked up suddenly. "A girl visited him here at the plant half a year ago. She was pretty, I suppose—blond and slim. And, of course, could scarcely add two and two. He spent all day puffing out his chest, trying to explain how a robot was put together." The hardness had returned. "Not that she understood! Who was she?"

Herbie answered without hesitation. "I know the person you are referring to. She is his first cousin, and there is no romantic interest there, I assure you."

Susan Calvin rose to her feet with a vivacity almost girlish. "Now isn't that strange? That's exactly what I used to pretend to myself sometimes, though I never really thought so. Then it all must be true."

She ran to Herbie and seized his cold, heavy hand in both hers. "Thank you, Herbie." Her voice was an urgent, husky whisper. "Don't tell anyone about this. Let it be our secret—and thank you again." With that, and a convulsive squeeze of Herbie's unresponsive metal fingers, she left.

Herbie turned slowly to his neglected novel, but there was no one to read *his* thoughts.

Milton Ashe stretched slowly and magnificently, to the tune of cracking joints and a chorus of grunts, and then glared at Peter Bogert, Ph.D.

"Say," he said, "I've been at this for a week now with just about no sleep. How long do I have to keep it up? I thought you said the positronic bombardment in Vac Chamber D was the solution."

Bogert yawned delicately and regarded his white hands with interest. "It is. I'm on the track."

"I know what *that* means when a mathematician says it. How near the end are you?"

"It all depends."

"On what?" Ashe dropped into a chair and stretched his long legs out before him.

"On Lanning. The old fellow disagrees with me." He sighed. "A bit behind the times, that's the trouble with him. He clings to matrix mechanics as the all in all, and this problem calls for more powerful mathematical tools. He's so stubborn."

Ashe muttered sleepily, "Why not ask Herbie and settle the whole affair?"

"Ask the robot?" Bogert's eyebrows climbed.

"Why not? Didn't the old girl tell you?"

"You mean Calvin?"

"Yeah! Susie herself. That robot's a mathematical wiz. He knows all about everything plus a bit on the side. He does triple integrals in his head and eats up tensor analysis for dessert."

The mathematician stared skeptically. "Are you serious?"

"So help me! The catch is that the dope doesn't like math. He would rather read slushy novels. Honest! You should see the tripe Susie keeps feeding him: 'Purple Passion' and 'Love in Space.'"

"Dr. Calvin hasn't said a word of this to us."

"Well, she hasn't finished studying him. You know how she is. She likes to have everything just so before letting out the big secret."

"She's told *you*."

"We sort of got to talking. I have been seeing a lot of her lately." He opened his eyes wide and frowned. "Say, Bogie, have you been noticing anything queer about the lady lately?"

Bogert relaxed into an undignified grin. "She's using lipstick, if that's what you mean."

"Hell, I know that. Rouge, powder and eye shadow, too. She's a sight. But it's not that. I can't put my finger on it. It's the way she talks—as if she were happy about something." He thought a little, and then shrugged.

The other allowed himself a leer, which, for a scientist past fifty, was not a bad job. "Maybe she's in love."

Ashe allowed his eyes to close again. "You're nuts, Bogie. You go speak to Herbie; I want to stay here and go to sleep."

"Right! Not that I particularly like having a robot tell me my job, nor that I think he can do it!"

A soft snore was his only answer.

Herbie listened carefully as Peter Bogert, hands in pockets, spoke with elaborate indifference.

"So there you are. I've been told you understand these things, and I am asking you more in curiosity than anything else. My line of reasoning, as I have outlined it, involves a few doubtful steps, I admit, which Dr. Lanning refuses to accept, and the picture is still rather incomplete."

The robot didn't answer, and Bogert said, "Well?"

"I see no mistake." Herbie studied the scribbled figures.

"I don't suppose you can go any further than that?"

"I daren't try. You are a better mathematician than I, and—well, I'd hate to commit myself."

There was a shade of complacency in Bogert's smile. "I rather thought that would be the case. It is deep. We'll forget it." He crumpled the sheets, tossed them down the waste shaft, turned to leave, and then thought better of it.

"By the way—"

The robot waited.

Bogert seemed to have difficulty. "There is something—that is, perhaps you can—" He stopped.

Herbie spoke quietly. "Your thoughts are confused, but there is no doubt at all that they concern Dr. Lanning. It is silly to hesitate, for as soon as you compose yourself, I'll know what it is you want to ask."

The mathematician's hand went to his sleek hair in the familiar smoothing gesture. "Lanning is nudging seventy," he said, as if that explained everything.

"I know that."

"And he's been director of the plant for almost thirty years." Herbie nodded.

"Well, now." Bogert's voice became ingratiating. "You would know whether . . . whether he's thinking of resigning. Health, perhaps, or some other—"

"Quite," said Herbie, and that was all.

"Well, do you know?"

"Certainly."

"Then—uh—could you tell me?"

"Since you ask, yes." The robot was quite matter-of-fact about it. "He has already resigned!"

"What!" The exclamation was an explosive, almost inarticulate, sound. The scientist's large head hunched forward. "Say that again!"

"He has already resigned," came the quiet repetition, "but it has not yet taken effect. He is waiting, you see, to solve the problem of—er—myself. That finished, he is quite ready to turn the office of director over to his successor."

Bogert expelled his breath sharply. "And this successor? Who is he?" He was quite close to Herbie now, eyes fixed fascinatedly on those unreadable dull-red photoelectric cells that were the robot's eyes.

Words came slowly. "You are the next director."

And Bogert relaxed into a tight smile. "This is good to know. I've been hoping and waiting for this. Thanks, Herbie."

Peter Bogert was at his desk until five that morning

and he was back at nine. The shelf just over the desk emptied of its row of reference books and tables, as he referred to one after the other. The pages of calculations before him increased microscopically and the crumpled sheets at his feet mounted into a hill of scribbled paper.

At precisely noon, he stared at the final page, rubbed a bloodshot eye, yawned and shrugged. "This is getting worse each minute. Damn!"

He turned at the sound of the opening door and nodded at Lanning, who entered, cracking the knuckles of one gnarled hand with the other.

The director took in the disorder of the room and his eyebrows furrowed together.

"New lead?" he asked.

"No," came the defiant answer. "What's wrong with the old one?"

Lanning did not trouble to answer, nor to do more than bestow a single cursory glance at the top sheet upon Bogert's desk. He spoke through the flare of a match as he lit a cigar.

"Has Calvin told you about the robot? It's a mathematical genius. Really remarkable."

The other snorted loudly. "So I've heard. But Calvin had better stick to robopsychology. I've checked Herbie on math, and he can scarcely struggle through calculus."

"Calvin didn't find it so."

"She's crazy."

"And I don't find it so." The director's eyes narrowed dangerously.

"You!" Bogert's voice hardened. "What are you talking about?"

"I've been putting Herbie through his paces all morning, and he can do tricks you never heard of."

"Is that so?"

"You sound skeptical!" Lanning flipped a sheet of paper out of his vest pocket and unfolded it. "That's not my handwriting, is it?"

Bogert studied the large angular notation covering the sheet. "Herbie did this?"

"Right! And if you'll notice, he's been working on your time integration of Equation 22. It comes"— Lanning tapped a yellow fingernail upon the last step —"to the identical conclusion I did, and in a quarter the time. You had no right to neglect the Linger Effect in positronic bombardment."

"I didn't neglect it. For Heaven's sake, Lanning, get it through your head that it would cancel out—"

"Oh, sure, you explained that. You used the Mitchell Translation Equation, didn't you? Well—it doesn't apply."

"Why not?"

"Because you've been using hyper-imaginaries, for one thing."

"What's that to do with?"

"Mitchell's Equation won't hold when—"

"Are you crazy? If you'll reread Mitchell's original paper in the *Transactions of the Far*—"

"I don't have to. I told you in the beginning that I didn't like his reasoning, and Herbie backs me in that."

"Well, then," Bogert shouted, "let that clockwork contraption solve the entire problem for you. Why bother with nonessentials?"

"That's exactly the point. Herbie can't solve the problem. And if he can't, we can't—alone. I'm submitting the entire question to the National Board. It's gotten beyond us."

Bogert's chair went over backward as he jumped up a-snarl, face crimson. "You're doing nothing of the sort."

Lanning flushed in his turn. "Are you telling me what I can't do?"

"Exactly," was the gritted response. "I've got the problem beaten and you're not to take it out of my hands, understand? Don't think I don't see through you, you desiccated fossil. You'd cut your own nose off before you'd let me get the credit for solving robotic telepathy."

"You're a damned idiot, Bogert, and in one second I'll have you suspended for insubordination." Lanning's lower lip trembled with passion.

"Which is one thing you won't do, Lanning. You haven't any secrets with a mind-reading robot around, so don't forget that I know all about your resignation."

The ash on Lanning's cigar trembled and fell, and the cigar itself followed. "What . . . what—"

Bogert chuckled nastily. "And I'm the new director, be it understood. I'm very aware of that; don't think I'm not. Damn your eyes, Lanning, I'm going to give the orders about here or there will be the sweetest mess that you've ever been in."

Lanning found his voice and let it out with a roar. "You're suspended, d'ye hear? You're relieved of all duties. You're broken, do you understand?"

The smile on the other's face broadened. "Now, what's the use of that? You're getting nowhere. I'm holding the trumps. I know you've resigned. Herbie told me, and he got it straight from you."

Lanning forced himself to speak quietly. He looked an old, old man, with tired eyes peering from a face in which the red had disappeared, leaving the pasty yellow of age behind. "I want to speak to Herbie. He can't have told you anything of the sort. You're playing a deep game, Bogert, but I'm calling your bluff. Come with me."

Bogert shrugged. "To see Herbie? Good! Damned good!"

It was also precisely at noon that Milton Ashe looked up from his clumsy sketch and said, "You get the idea? I'm not too good at getting this down, but that's about how it looks. It's a honey of a house, and I can get it for next to nothing."

Susan Calvin gazed across at him with melting eyes. "It's really beautiful," she sighed. "I've often thought that I'd like to . . ." Her voice trailed away.

"Of course," Ashe continued briskly, putting away his pencil, "I've got to wait for my vacation. It's only two weeks off, but this Herbie business has everything up in the air." His eyes dropped to his fingernails. "Besides, there's another point—but it's a secret."

"Then don't tell me."

"Oh, I'd just as soon, I'm just busting to tell someone—and you're just about the best—er—confidante
I could find here." He grinned sheepishly.

Susan Calvin's heart bounded, but she did not trust
herself to speak.

"Frankly," Ashe scraped his chair closer and lowered
his voice into a confidential whisper, "the house isn't
to be only for myself. I'm getting married!"

And then he jumped out of his seat. "What's the
matter?"

"Nothing!" The horrible spinning sensation had vanished, but it was hard to get words out. "Married? You
mean—"

"Why, sure! About time, isn't it? You remember that
girl who was here last summer? That's she! But you
are sick. You—"

"Headache!" Susan Calvin motioned him away
weakly. "I've . . . I've been subject to them lately. I
want to . . . to congratulate you, of course. I'm very
glad—" The inexpertly applied rouge made a pair of
nasty red splotches upon her chalk-white face.
Things had begun spinning again. "Pardon me—
please—"

The words were a mumble as she stumbled blindly
out the door. It had happened with the sudden catastrophe of a dream—and with all the unreal horror of
a dream.

But how could it be? Herbie had said—

And Herbie knew! He could see into minds!

She found herself leaning breathlessly against the door jamb, staring into Herbie's metal face. She must have climbed the two flights of stairs, but she had no memory of it. The distance had been covered in an instant, as in a dream.

As in a dream!

And still Herbie's unblinking eyes stared into hers and their dull red seemed to expand into dimly shining nightmarish globes.

He was speaking, and she felt the cold glass pressing against her lips. She swallowed and shuddered into a certain awareness of her surroundings.

Still Herbie spoke, and there was agitation in his voice—as if he were hurt and frightened and pleading.

The words were beginning to make sense. "This is a dream," he was saying, "and you mustn't believe in it. You'll wake into the real world soon and laugh at yourself. He loves you, I tell you. He does, he does! But not here! Not now! This is an illusion."

Susan Calvin nodded, her voice a whisper. "Yes! Yes!" She was clutching Herbie's arm, clinging to it, repeating over and over, "It isn't true, is it? It isn't, is it?"

Just how she came to her senses, she never knew —but it was like passing from a world of misty unreality to one of harsh sunlight. She pushed him away from her, pushed hard against the steely arm, and her eyes were wide.

"What are you trying to do?" Her voice rose to a harsh scream. "What are you trying to do?"

Herbie backed away. "I want to help."

The psychologist stared. "Help? By telling me this is a dream? By trying to push me into schizophrenia?" A hysterical tenseness seized her. "This is no dream! I wish it were!"

She drew her breath sharply, "Wait! Why . . . why, I understand. Merciful heavens, it's so obvious."

There was horror in the robot's voice. "I had to!"

"And I believed you! I never thought—"

Loud voices outside the door brought her to a halt. She turned away, fists clenching spasmodically, and when Bogert and Lanning entered, she was at the far window. Neither of the men paid her the slightest attention.

They approached Herbie simultaneously; Lanning angry and impatient, Bogert, coolly sardonic. The director spoke first.

"Here now, Herbie. Listen to me!"

The robot brought his eyes sharply down upon the aged director. "Yes, Dr. Lanning."

"Have you discussed me with Dr. Bogert?"

"No, sir." The answer came slowly, and the smile on Bogert's face flashed off.

"What's that?" Bogert shoved in ahead of his superior and straddled the ground before the robot. "Repeat what you told me yesterday."

"I said that—" Herbie fell silent. Deep within him his metallic diaphragm vibrated in soft discords.

"Didn't you say he had resigned?" roared Bogert. "Answer me!"

Bogert raised his arm frantically, but Lanning pushed him aside. "Are you trying to bully him into lying?"

"You heard him, Lanning. He began to say 'Yes' and stopped. Get out of my way! I want the truth out of him, understand!"

"I'll ask him!" Lanning turned to the robot. "All right, Herbie, take it easy. Have I resigned?"

Herbie stared, and Lanning repeated anxiously, "Have I resigned?" There was the faintest trace of a negative shake of the robot's head. A long wait produced nothing further.

The two men looked at each other and the hostility in their eyes was all but tangible.

"What the devil," blurted Bogert, "has the robot gone mute? Can't you speak, you monstrosity?"

"I can speak," came the ready answer.

"Then answer the question. Didn't you tell me Lanning had resigned? Hasn't he resigned?"

And again there was nothing but dull silence, until, from the end of the room, Susan Calvin's laugh rang out suddenly, high-pitched and semi-hysterical.

The two mathematicians jumped, and Bogert's eyes narrowed. "You here? What's so funny?"

"Nothing's funny." Her voice was not quite natural. "It's just that I'm not the only one that's been caught. There's irony in three of the greatest experts in robotics in the world falling into the same elementary trap, isn't there?" Her voice faded, and she put a pale hand to her forehead. "But it isn't funny!"

This time the look that passed between the two men was one of raised eyebrows. "What trap are you talking about?" asked Lanning stiffly. "Is something wrong with Herbie?"

"No." She approached them slowly. "Nothing is wrong with him—only with us." She whirled suddenly and shrieked at the robot, "Get away from me! Go to the other end of the room and don't let me look at you."

Herbie cringed before the fury of her eyes and stumbled away in a clattering trot.

Lanning's voice was hostile. "What is all this, Dr. Calvin?"

She faced them and spoke sarcastically, "Surely you know the fundamental First Law of Robotics."

The other two nodded together. "Certainly," said Bogert, irritably. "A robot may not injure a human being or, through inaction, allow him to come to harm."

"How nicely put," sneered Calvin. "But what kind of harm?"

"Why—any kind."

"Exactly! Any kind! But what about hurt feelings? What about deflation of one's ego? What about the blasting of one's hopes? Is that injury?"

Lanning frowned. "What would a robot know about—" And then he caught himself with a gasp.

"You've caught on, have you? *This* robot reads minds. Do you suppose it doesn't know everything about mental injury? Do you suppose that if asked a question, it wouldn't give exactly that answer that one wants to hear? Wouldn't any other answer hurt us, and wouldn't Herbie know that?"

"Good heavens!" muttered Bogert.

The psychologist cast a sardonic glance at him. "I take it you asked him whether Lanning had resigned. You wanted to hear that he had resigned and so that's what Herbie told you."

"And I suppose that is why," said Lanning, tonelessly, "it would not answer a little while ago. It couldn't answer either way without hurting one of us."

There was a short pause in which the men looked thoughtfully across the room at the robot, crouching in the chair by the bookcase, head resting in one hand.

Susan Calvin stared steadfastly at the floor. "He knew of all this. That . . . that devil knows everything—including what went wrong in his assembly." Her eyes were dark and brooding.

Lanning looked up, "You're wrong there, Dr. Calvin. He doesn't know what went wrong. I asked him."

"What does that mean?" cried Calvin. "Only that you didn't want him to give you the solution. It would puncture your ego to have a machine do what you couldn't. Did you ask him?" she shot at Bogert.

"In a way." Bogert coughed and reddened. "He told me he knew very little about mathematics."

Lanning laughed, not very loudly, and the psychologist smiled caustically. She said, "I'll ask him! A solution by him won't hurt my ego." She raised her voice into a cold, imperative, "Come here!"

Herbie rose and approached with hesitant steps.

"You know, I suppose," she continued, "just exactly at what point in the assembly an extraneous factor was introduced or an essential one left out."

"Yes," said Herbie, in tones barely heard.

"Hold on," broke in Bogert angrily. "That's not necessarily true. You want to hear that, that's all."

"Don't be a fool," replied Calvin. "He certainly knows as much math as you and Lanning together, since he can read minds. Give him his chance."

The mathematician subsided, and Calvin continued, "All right, then, Herbie, give! We're waiting." And in an aside, "Get pencils and paper, gentlemen."

But Herbie remained silent, and there was triumph in the psychologist's voice. "Why don't you answer, Herbie?"

The robot blurted out suddenly, "I cannot. You know I cannot! Dr. Bogert and Dr. Lanning don't want me to."

"They want the solution."

"But not from me."

Lanning broke in, speaking slowly and distinctly, "Don't be foolish, Herbie. We do want you to tell us."

Bogert nodded curtly.

Herbie's voice rose to wild heights. "What's the use of saying that? Don't you suppose that I can see past the superficial skin of your mind? Down below, you don't want me to. I'm a machine, given the imitation of life only by virtue of the positronic interplay in my brain—which is man's device. You can't lose face to me without being hurt. That is deep in your mind and won't be erased. I can't give the solution."

"We'll leave," said Dr. Lanning. "Tell Calvin."

"That would make no difference," cried Herbie, "since you would know anyway that it was I that was supplying the answer."

Calvin resumed, "But you understand, Herbie, that despite that, Drs. Lanning and Bogert want that solution."

"By their own efforts!" insisted Herbie.

"But they want it, and the fact that you have it and won't give it hurts them. You see that, don't you?"

"Yes! Yes!"

"And if you tell them that will hurt them, too."

"Yes! Yes!" Herbie was retreating slowly, and step by step Susan Calvin advanced. The two men watched in frozen bewilderment.

"You can't tell them," droned the psychologist slowly, "because that would hurt and you mustn't hurt. But if you don't tell them, you hurt, so you must tell them. And if you do, you will hurt and you mustn't, so you can't tell them; but if you don't, you hurt, so you must; but if you do, you hurt, so you mustn't; but if you don't, you hurt, so you must; but if you do, you—"

Herbie was up against the wall, and here he dropped to his knees. "Stop!" he shrieked. "Close your mind! It is full of pain and frustration and hate! I didn't mean it, I tell you! I tried to help! I told you what you wanted to hear. I had to!"

The psychologist paid no attention. "You must tell them, but if you do, you hurt, so you mustn't; but if you don't, you hurt, so you must; but—"

And Herbie screamed!

It was like the whistling of a piccolo many times magnified—shrill and shriller till it keened with the terror of a lost soul and filled the room with the piercingness of itself.

And when it died into nothingness, Herbie collapsed into a huddled heap of motionless metal.

Bogert's face was bloodless. "He's dead!"

"No!" Susan Calvin burst into body-racking gusts of wild laughter. "Not dead—merely insane. I confronted him with the insoluble dilemma, and he broke down. You can scrap him now—because he'll never speak again."

Lanning was on his knees beside the thing that had been Herbie. His fingers touched the cold, unresponsive metal face and he shuddered. "You did that on purpose." He rose and faced her, face contorted.

"What if I did? You can't help it now." And in a sudden access of bitterness, "He deserved it."

The director seized the paralyzed, motionless Bogert by the wrist. "What's the difference. Come, Peter." He sighed. "A thinking robot of this type is worthless anyway." His eyes were old and tired, and he repeated, "Come, Peter!"

It was minutes after the two scientists left that Dr. Susan Calvin regained part of her mental equilibrium. Slowly, her eyes turned to the living-dead Herbie and the tightness returned to her face. Long she stared while the triumph faded and the helpless frustration returned—and of all her turbulent thoughts only one infinitely bitter word passed her lips.

"Liar!"

Something Wild Is Loose . . .

BY ROBERT SILVERBERG

Suppose a creature from a world where everyone communicates telepathically suddenly found itself transported to Earth, a world where there are no telepaths at all (or hardly any). Suppose the creature from another planet happened to be invisible, and frightened, and desperately eager to go home. Suppose, in its fear and loneliness, it attempted to make contact with the minds of the human beings all about it. How would they react? With sympathy—or with terror?

1.

*T*he Vsiir got aboard the Earthbound ship
by accident. It had absolutely no plans for taking a
holiday on a wet, grimy planet like Earth. But it was in
its metamorphic phase, undergoing the period of un-
disciplined change that began as winter came on, and
it had shifted so far up-spectrum that Earthborn eyes
couldn't see it. Oh, a really skilled observer might notice a slippery little purple flicker once in a while, a
kind of snore, as the Vsiir momentarily dropped down
out of the ultraviolet; but he'd have to know where to
look, and when. The crewman who was responsible for
putting the Vsiir on the ship never even considered the
possibility that there might be something invisible
sleeping atop one of the crates of cargo being hoisted
into the ship's hold. He simply went down the row,
slapping a floater-node on each crate and sending it
gliding up the gravity well toward the open hatch. The
fifth crate to go inside was the one on which the Vsiir
had decided to take its nap. The spaceman didn't
know that he had inadvertently given an alien organism a free ride to Earth. The Vsiir didn't know it,
either, until the hatch was sealed and an oxygen-nitrogen atmosphere began to hiss from the vents. The
Vsiir did not happen to breathe those gases, but, because it was in its time of metamorphosis, it was able
to adapt itself quickly and nicely to the sour, prickly
vapors seeping into its metabolic cells. The next step
was to fashion a set of full-spectrum scanners and

learn something about its surroundings. Within a few minutes, the Vsiir was aware—

—that it was in a large, dark place that held a great many boxes containing various mineral and vegetable products of its world, mainly branches of the green-fire tree but also some other things of no comprehensible value to a Vsiir—

—that a double wall of curved metal enclosed this place—

—that just beyond this wall was a null-atmosphere zone, such as is found between one planet and another—

—that this entire closed system was undergoing acceleration—

—that this therefore was a spaceship, heading rapidly away from the world of Vsiirs and in fact already some ten planetary diameters distant, with the gap growing alarmingly moment by moment—

—that it would be impossible, even for a Vsiir in metamorphosis, to escape from the spaceship at this point—

—and that, unless it could persuade the crew of the ship to halt and go back, it would be compelled to undertake a long and dreary voyage to a strange and probably loathsome world, where life would at best be highly inconvenient, and might present great dangers. It would find itself cut off painfully from the rhythm of its own civilization. It would miss the Festival of Changing. It would miss the Holy Eclipse. It would not be able to take part in next spring's Rising of the Sea. It would suffer in a thousand ways.

There were six human beings aboard the ship. Extending its perceptors, the Vsiir tried to reach their
minds. Though humans had been coming to its planet
for many years, it had never bothered making contact
with them before; but it had never been in this much
trouble before, either. It sent a foggy tendril of thought
roving the corridors, looking for traces of human intelligence. Here? A glow of electrical activity within a
sphere of bone: a mind, a mind! A busy mind. But
surrounded by a wall, apparently; the Vsiir rammed up
against it and was thrust back. That was startling and
disturbing. What kind of beings were these, whose
minds were closed to ordinary contact? The Vsiir went
on, hunting through the ship. Another mind: again
closed. Another. Another. The Vsiir felt panic rising.
Its mantle fluttered; its energy radiations dropped far
down into the visual spectrum, then shot nervously
toward much shorter waves. Even its physical form experienced a series of quick, involuntary metamor-
phoses, to the Vsiir's intense embarrassment. It did not
get control of its body until it had passed from spherical to cubical to chaotic, and had become a gridwork
of fibrous threads held together only by a pulsing
strand of ego. Fiercely it forced itself back to the spherical form and resumed its search of the ship, dismally
realizing that by now its native world was half a solar
unit away. It was without hope now, but it continued
to probe the minds of the crew, if only for the sake of
thoroughness. Even if it made contact, though,
how could it communicate the nature of its plight,
and even if it communicated, why would the humans

be disposed to help it? Yet it went on through the ship. And—

Here: an open mind. No wall at all. A miracle! The Vsiir rushed into close contact, overcome with joy and surprise, pouring out its predicament. *Please listen. Unfortunate non-human organism accidentally transported into this vessel during loading of cargo. Metabolically and psychologically unsuited for prolonged life on Earth. Begs pardon for inconvenience, wishes prompt return to home planet recently left, regrets disturbance in shipping schedule but hopes that this large favor will not prove impossible to grant. Do you comprehend my sending? Unfortunate non-human organism accidentally transported—*

2.

Lieutenant Falkirk had drawn the first sleep-shift after floatoff. It was only fair; Falkirk had knocked himself out processing the cargo during the loading stage, slapping the floater-nodes on every crate and feeding the transit manifests to the computer. Now that the ship was spaceborne he could grab some rest while the other crewmen were handling the floatoff chores. So he settled down for six hours in the cradle as soon as they were on their way. Below him, the ship's six gravity-drinkers spun on their axes, gobbling inertia and pushing up the acceleration, and the ship floated Earthward at a velocity that would reach the galactic level before Falkirk woke. He drifted into drowsiness. A good trip: enough green-fire bark in the hold to see Earth through a dozen fits of the molecule plague, and plenty of other potential medicinals besides, along with a load of interesting mineral samples, and—Falkirk slept. For half an hour he enjoyed sweet slumber, his mind disengaged, his body loose.

Until a dark dream bubbled through his skull.

Deep purple sunlight, hot and somber. Something slippery tickling the edges of his brain. He lies on a broad white slab in a scorched desert. Unable to move. Getting harder to breathe. The gravity—a terrible pull, bending and breaking him, ripping his bones apart. Hooded figures moving around him, pointing, laughing, exchanging blurred comments in an unknown language. His skin melting and taking on a new texture: porcupine quills sprouting inside his flesh and forcing their way upward, poking out through every pore. Points of fire all over him. A thin scarlet hand, withered red fingers like crab-claws, hovering in front of his face. Scratching. Scratching. Scratching. His blood running among the quills, thick and sluggish. He shivers, struggling to sit up—lifts a hand, leaving pieces of quivering flesh stuck to the slab —sits up—

Wakes, trembling, screaming.

Falkirk's shout still sounded in his ears as his eyes adjusted to the light. Lieutenant Commander Rodriguez was holding his shoulders and shaking him.

"You all right?"

Falkirk tried to reply. Words wouldn't come. Hallucinatory shock, he realized, as part of his mind attempted to convince the other part that the dream was over. He was trained to handle crises: he ran through a quick disciplinary countdown and calmed himself, though he was still badly shaken. "Nightmare," he said hoarsely. "A beauty. Never had a dream with that kind of intensity before."

Rodriguez relaxed. Obviously he couldn't get very upset over a mere nightmare. "You want a pill?"

Falkirk shook his head. "I'll manage, thanks."

But the impact of the dream lingered. It was more than an hour before he got back to sleep, and then he fell into a light, restless doze, as if his mind were on guard against a return of those chilling fantasies. Fifty minutes before his programmed wake-up time, he was awakened by a ghastly shriek from the far side of the cabin.

Lieutenant Commander Rodriguez was having a nightmare.

3.

When the ship made floatdown on Earth a month later, it was, of course, put through the usual decontamination procedures before anyone or anything aboard it was allowed out of the starport. The outer hull got squirted with sealants designed to trap and smother any microorganism that might have hitchhiked from another world; the crewmen emerged through the safety pouch and went straight into a quarantine chamber without being exposed to the air; the ship's atmosphere was cycled into withdrawal chambers, where it underwent a thorough purification, and the entire interior of the vessel received a six-phase sterilization, beginning with fifteen minutes of hard vacuum and ending with an hour of neutron bombardment.

These procedures caused a certain degree of inconvenience for the Vsiir. It was already at the low end of its energy phase, due mainly to the repeated discouragements it had suffered in its attempts to communicate with the six humans. Now it was forced to adapt to a variety of unpleasant environments with no chance to rest between changes. Even the most adaptable of organisms can get tired. By the time the starport's decontamination team was ready to certify that the ship was wholly free of alien life-forms, the Vsiir was very, very tired indeed.

The oxygen-nitrogen atmosphere entered the hold once more. The Vsiir found it quite welcome, at least in contrast to all that had just been thrown at it. The hatch was open; stevedores were muscling the cargo crates into position to be floated across the field to the handling dome. The Vsiir took advantage of this moment to extrude some legs and scramble out of the ship. It found itself on a broad concrete apron rimmed by massive buildings. A yellow sun was shining in a blue sky; infrared was bouncing all over the place, but the Vsiir speedily made arrangements to deflect the excess. It also compensated immediately for the tinge of ugly hydrocarbons in the atmosphere, for the frightening noise level, and for the leaden feeling of homesickness that suddenly threatened its organic stabilitv at the first sight of this unfamiliar, disheartening world. How to get home again? How to make contact, even? The Vsiir sensed nothing but closed minds—sealed like seeds in their shells. True, from time to time the minds of these humans opened, but even then they seemed unwilling to let the Vsiir's message get through.

Perhaps it would be different here. Perhaps those six were poor communicators, for some reason, and there would be more receptive minds available in this place. Perhaps. Perhaps. Close to despair, the Vsiir hurried across the field, and slipped into the first building in which it sensed open minds. There were hundreds of humans in it, occupying many levels, and the open minds were widely scattered. The Vsiir located the nearest one and, worriedly, earnestly, hopefully, touched the tip of its mind to the human's. *Please listen. I mean no harm. Am non-human organism arrived on your planet through unhappy circumstances, wishing only quick going back to own world—*

4.

The cardiac wing of Long Island Starport Hospital was on the ground floor, in the rear, where the patients could be given floater therapy without upsetting the gravitational ratios of the rest of the building. As always, the hospital was full—people were always coming in sick off starliners, and most of them were hospitalized right at the starport for their own safety— and the cardiac wing had more than its share. At the moment it held a dozen infarcts awaiting implant, nine post-implant recupes, five coronaries in emergency stasis, three ventricle-regrowth projects, an aortal patch job, and nine or ten assorted other cases. Most of the patients were floating, to keep down the gravitational strain on their damaged tissues—all but the regrowth people, who were under full Earthnorm gravity so that their new hearts would come in with the proper resilience and toughness. The hospital had a fine reputation and one of the lowest mortality rates in the hemisphere.

Losing two patients the same morning was a shock to the entire staff.

At 0917 the monitor flashed the red light for Mrs. Maldonado, eighty-seven, post-transplant and thus far doing fine. She had developed acute endocarditis coming back from a tour of the Jupiter system; at her age there wasn't enough vitality to sustain her through the slow business of growing a new heart with a genetic prod, but they'd given her a synthetic implant and for two weeks it had worked quite well. Suddenly, though, the hospital control center was getting a load of grim telemetry from Mrs. Maldonado's bed: valve action zero, blood pressure zero, respiration zero, pulse zero, everything zero, zero, zero. The EEG showed a violent lurch, as though she had received some abrupt and intense shock, followed by a minute or two of irregular action, followed by termination of brain activity. Long before any hospital personnel had reached her bedside, automatic revival equipment, both chemical and electrical, had gone to work on the patient, but she was beyond reach: a massive cerebral hemorrhage, coming totally without warning, had done irreversible damage.

At 0928 came the second outage: Mr. Guinness, fifty-one, three days past surgery for a coronary embolism. The same series of events. A severe jolt to the nervous system, an immediate and fatal physiological response. Resuscitation procedures negative. No one on the staff had any plausible explanation for Mr. Guinness' death. Like Mrs. Maldonado, he had been sleeping peacefully, all vital signs good, until the moment of the fatal seizure.

"As though someone had come up and yelled *boo* in their ears," one doctor muttered, puzzling over the charts. He pointed to the wild EEG track. "Or as if they'd had unbearably vivid nightmares and couldn't take the sensory overload. But no one was making noise in the ward. And nightmares aren't contagious."

5.

Dr. Peter Mookherji, resident in neuropathology, was beginning his morning rounds on the hospital's sixth level when the soft voice of his annunciator, taped behind his left ear, asked him to report to the Quarantine Building immediately. Dr. Mookherji scowled. "Can't it wait? This is my busiest time of day, and—"

"You are asked to come at once."

"Look, I've got a girl in a coma here, due for her teletherapy session in fifteen minutes, and she's counting on seeing me. I'm her only link to the world. If I'm not there when—"

"You are asked to come at once, Dr. Mookherji."

"Why do the quarantine people need a neuropathologist in such a hurry? Let me take care of the girl, at least, and in forty-five minutes they can have me."

"Dr. Mookherji—"

It didn't pay to argue with a machine. Mookherji forced his temper down. Short tempers ran in his family, along with a fondness for torrid curries and a talent for telepathy. Glowering, he grabbed a data terminal, identified himself, and told the hospital's control center to reprogram his entire morning schedule. "Build in a half-hour postponement somehow," he snapped. "I can't help it—see for yourself. I've been requisitioned by the quarantine staff." The computer was thoughtful enough to have a rollerbuggy waiting for him when he emerged from the hospital. It whisked him across the starport to the Quarantine Building in three minutes, but he was still angry when he got there. The scanner at the door ticked off his badge and one of the control center's innumerable voice-outputs told him solemnly, "You are expected in Room 403, Dr. Mookherji."

Room 403 turned out to be a two-sector interrogation office. The rear sector of the room was part of the building's central quarantine core, and the front sector belonged to the public-access part of the building, with a thick glass wall in between. Six haggard-looking spacemen were slouched on sofas behind the wall, and three members of the starport's quarantine staff paced about in the front. Mookherji's irritation ebbed when he saw that one of the quarantine men was an old medical-school friend, Lee Nakadai. The slender Japanese was a year older than Mookherji— twenty-nine to twenty-eight; they met for lunch occasionally at the starport commissary, and they had double-dated a pair of Filipino twins earlier in the year, but the pressure of work had kept them apart for months. Nakadai got down to business quickly now. "Pete, have you ever heard of an epidemic of nightmares?"

Indicating the men behind the quarantine wall, Nakadai said, "These fellows came in an hour and a half ago from Norton's Star. Brought back a cargo of green-fire bark. Physically they check out to five decimal places, and I'd release them except for one funny thing. They're all in a bad state of nervous exhaustion, which they say is the result of having had practically no sleep during their whole month-long return trip. And the reason for that is that they were having nightmares—every one of them—real mind-wrecking killer dreams, whenever they tried to sleep. It sounded so peculiar that I thought we'd better run a neuropath checkup, in case they've picked up some kind of cerebral infection."

Mookherji frowned. "For this you get me out of my ward on emergency requisition, Lee?"

"Talk to them," Nakadai said. "Maybe it'll scare you a little."

Mookherji glanced at the spacemen. "All right," he said. "What about these nightmares?"

A tall, bony-looking officer who introduced himself as Lieutenant Falkirk said, "I was the first victim—right after floatoff. I almost flipped. It was like, well, something touching my mind, filling it with weird thoughts. And everything absolutely real while it was going on—I thought I was choking, I thought my body was changing into something alien, I felt my blood running out my pores—" Falkirk shrugged. "Like any sort of bad dream, I guess, only ten times as vivid. Fifty times. A few hours later Lieutenant Commander Rodriguez had the same kind of dream. Different images, same effect. And then, one by one, as the others took their sleep-shifts, they started to wake up screaming. Two of us ended up spending three weeks on happy-pills. We're pretty stable men, doctor—we're trained to take almost anything. But I think a civilian would have cracked up for good with dreams like those. Not so much the images as the intensity, the realness of it."

"And these dreams recurred throughout the voyage?" Mookherji asked.

"Every shift. It got so we were afraid to doze off, because we knew the devils would start crawling through our heads when we did. Or we'd put ourselves real down on sleeper-tabs. And even so we'd have the dreams, with our minds doped to a level where you wouldn't imagine dreams would happen. A plague of nightmares, doctor. An epidemic."

"When was the last episode?"

"The final sleep-shift before floatdown."

"You haven't gone to sleep, any of you, since leaving the ship?"

"No," Falkirk said.

One of the other spacemen said, "Maybe he didn't make it clear to you, doctor. These were killer dreams. They were mind-crackers. We were lucky to get home sane. If we did."

Mookherji drummed his fingertips together, rummaging through his experience for some parallel case. He couldn't find any. He knew of mass hallucinations, plenty of them, episodes in which whole mobs had persuaded themselves they had seen gods, demons, miracles, the dead walking, fiery symbols in the sky. But a series of hallucinations coming in sequence, shift after shift, to an entire crew of tough, pragmatic spacemen? It didn't make sense.

Nakadai said, "Pete, the men had a guess about what might have done it to them. Just a wild idea, but maybe—"

"What is it?"

Falkirk laughed uneasily. "Actually, it's pretty fantastic, doctor."

"Go ahead."

"Well, that something from the planet came aboard the ship with us. Something, well, telepathic. Which fiddled around with our minds whenever we went to sleep. What we felt as nightmares was maybe this thing inside our heads."

"Possibly it rode all the way back to Earth with us," another spaceman said. "It could still be aboard the ship. Or loose in the city by now."

"The Invisible Nightmare Menace?" Mookherji said, with a faint smile. "I doubt that I can buy that."

"There *are* telepathic creatures," Falkirk pointed out.

"I know," Mookherji said sharply. "I happen to be one myself."

"I'm sorry, doctor, if—"

"But that doesn't lead me to look for telepaths under every bush. I'm not ruling out your alien menace, mind you. But I think it's a lot more likely that you picked up some kind of inflammation of the brain out there. A virus disease, a type of encephalitis that shows itself in the form of chronic hallucinations." The spacemen looked troubled. Obviously they would rather be victims of an unknown monster preying on them from outside than of an unknown virus lodged in their brains. Mookherji went on, "I'm not saying that's what it is, either. I'm just tossing around hypotheses. We'll know more after we've run some tests." Checking his watch, he said to Nakadai, "Lee, there's not much more I can find out right now, and

I've got to get back to my patients. I want these fellows plugged in for the full series of neuropsychological checkouts. Have the outputs relayed to my office as they come in. Run the tests in staggered series and start letting the men go to sleep, two at a time, after each series—I'll send over a technician to help you rig the telemetry. I want to be notified immediately if there's any nightmare experience."

"Right."

"And get them to sign telepathy releases. I'll give them a preliminary mind-probe this evening after I've had a chance to study the clinical findings. Maintain absolute quarantine, of course. This thing might just be infectious. Play it very safe."

Nakadai nodded. Mookherji flashed a professional smile at the six somber spacemen and went out, brooding. A nightmare virus? Or a mind-meddling alien organism that no one can see? He wasn't sure which notion he liked less. Probably, though, there was some prosaic and unstartling explanation for that month of bad dreams—contaminated food supplies, or something funny in the atmosphere recycler. A simple, mundane explanation.

Probably.

6.

The first time it happened, the Vsiir was not sure what had actually taken place. It had touched a hu-

man mind; there had been an immediate vehement
reaction; the Vsiir had pulled back, alarmed by the
surging fury of the response, and then, a moment
later, had been unable to locate the mind at all. Possibly it was some defense mechanism, the Vsiir
thought, by which the humans guarded their minds
against intruders. But that made little sense, since the
humans' minds were quite effectively guarded most
of the time anyway. Aboard the ship, whenever the
Vsiir had managed to slip past the walls that shielded
the minds of the crewmen, it had always encountered a great deal of turbulence—plainly these humans did not enjoy mental contact with a Vsiir—but
never this complete shutdown, this total cutoff of
signal. Puzzled, the Vsiir tried again, reaching toward
an open mind situated not far from where the
one that had vanished had been. *Kindly attention, a
moment of consideration for confused otherworldly
individual, victim of unhappy circumstances, who—*
Again the violent response: a sudden tremendous
flare of mental energy, a churning blaze of fear and
pain and shock. And again, moments later, complete
silence, as though the human had retreated behind an
impermeable barrier. *Where are you? Where did you
go?* The Vsiir, troubled, took the risk of creating an
optical receptor that worked in the visual spectrum—
and that therefore would itself be visible to humans
—and surveyed the scene. It saw a human on a bed,
completely surrounded by intricate machinery. Col-
ored lights were flashing. Other humans, looking agi-

tated, were rushing toward the bed. The human on the bed lay quite still, not even moving when a metal arm descended and jabbed a long bright needle into his chest.

Suddenly the Vsiir understood.

The two humans must have experienced termination of existence!

Hastily the Vsiir dissolved its visual-spectrum receptor and retreated to a sheltered corner to consider what had happened. *Datum:* two humans had died. *Datum:* each had undergone termination immediately after receiving a mental transmission from the Vsiir. *Problem:* had the mental transmission brought about the terminations?

The possibility that the Vsiir might have destroyed two lives was shocking and appalling, and such a chill went through its body that it shrank into a tight, hard ball, with all thought-processes snarled. It needed several minutes to return to a fully functional state. If its attempts at communicating with these humans produced such terrible effects, the Vsiir realized, then its prospects of finding help on this planet were slim. How could it dare risk trying to contact other humans, if—

A comforting thought surfaced. The Vsiir realized that it was jumping to a hasty conclusion on the basis of sketchy evidence, while overlooking some powerful arguments against that conclusion. All during the voyage to this world the Vsiir had been making contact with humans, the six crewmen, and none of *them* had terminated. That was ample evidence that humans could withstand contact with a Vsiir mind. Therefore contact alone could not have caused these two deaths.

Possibly it was only coincidental that the Vsiir had approached two humans in succession that were on the verge of termination. Was this the place where humans were brought when their time of termination was near? Would the terminations have happened even if the Vsiir had not tried to make contact? Was the attempt at contact just enough of a drain on dwindling energies to push the two over the edge into termination? The Vsiir did not know. It was uncomfortably conscious of how many important facts it lacked. Only one thing was certain: its time was running short. If it did not find help soon, metabolic decay was going to set in, followed by metamorphic rigidity, followed by a fatal loss in adaptability, followed by . . . termination.

The Vsiir had no choice. Continuing its quest for contact with a human was its only hope of survival. Cautiously, timidly, the Vsiir again began to send out its probes, looking for a properly receptive mind. This one was walled. So was this. And all these: no entrance, no entrance! The Vsiir wondered if the barriers these humans possessed were designed merely to keep out intruding non-human consciousnesses, or actually shielded each human against mental contact of all kinds, including contact with other humans. If any human-to-human contact existed, the Vsiir had not detected it, either in this building or aboard the space-ship. What a strange race!

Perhaps it would be best to try a different level of this building. The Vsiir flowed easily under a closed door and up a service staircase to a higher floor. Once more it sent forth its probes. A closed mind here. And here. And here. And then a receptive one. The Vsiir prepared to send its message. For safety's sake it stepped down the power of its transmission, letting a mere wisp of thought curl forth. *Do you hear? Stranded extraterrestrial being is calling. Seeks aid. Wishes—*

From the human came a sharp, stinging displea-sure-response, wordless but unmistakably hostile. The Vsiir at once withdrew. It waited, terrified, fear-ing that it had caused another termination. No: the human mind continued to function, although it was no longer open, but surrounded by the sort of barrier humans normally wore. Drooping, dejected, the Vsiir crept away. Failure, again. Not even a moment of meaningful mind-to-mind contact. Was there no way to reach these people? Dismally, the Vsiir resumed its search for a receptive mind. What else could it do?

7.

The visit to the quarantine building had taken forty minutes out of Dr. Mookherji's morning schedule. That bothered him. He couldn't blame the quarantine people for getting upset over the six spacemen's tale of chronic hallucinations, but he didn't think the situation, mysterious as it was, was grave enough to warrant calling him in on an emergency basis. Whatever was troubling the spacemen would eventually come to light; meanwhile they were safely isolated from the rest of the starport. Nakadai should have run more tests before bothering him. And he resented having to steal time from his patients.

But as he began his belated morning rounds, Mookherji calmed himself with a deliberate effort: it wouldn't do him or his patients any good if he visited them while still loaded with tensions and irritations. He was supposed to be a healer, not a spreader of anxieties. He spent a moment going through a de-escalation routine, and by the time he entered the first patient's room—that of Satina Ransom—he was convincingly relaxed and amiable.

Satina lay on her left side, eyes closed, a slender girl of sixteen with a fragile-looking face and long, soft, straw-colored hair. A spidery network of monitoring systems surrounded her. She had been unconscious for sixteen months, twelve of them here in the starport's neuropathology ward and the last six under Mookherji's care. As a holiday treat, her parents had taken her to one of the resorts on Titan during the best season for viewing Saturn's rings; with great difficulty they had succeeded in booking reservations at Galileo Dome, and were there on the grim day when a violent Titanquake ruptured the dome and exposed a thousand tourists to the icy moon's poisonous methane atmosphere. Satina was one of the lucky ones: she got no more than a couple of whiffs of the stuff before a dome guide with whom she'd been talking managed to get a breathing mask over her face. She survived. Her mother, father, and younger brother didn't. But she had never regained consciousness after collapsing at the moment of the disaster. Months of examination on Earth had shown that her brief methane inhalation hadn't caused any major brain damage; organically there seemed to be nothing wrong with her, but she refused to wake up. A shock reaction, Mookherji believed: she would rather go on dreaming forever than return to the living nightmare that consciousness had become. He had been able to reach her mind telepathically, but so far he had been unable to cleanse her of the trauma of that catastrophe and bring her back to the waking world.

Now he prepared to make contact. There was nothing easy or automatic about his telepathy; "reading" minds was strenuous work for him, as difficult and as taxing as running a cross-country race or memorizing a lengthy part in *Hamlet*. Despite the fears of laymen, he had no way of scanning anyone's intimate thoughts with a casual glance. To enter another mind, he had to go through an elaborate procedure of warming up and reaching out, and even so it was a slow business to tune in on somebody's "wavelength," with little coherent information coming across until the ninth or tenth attempt. The gift had been in the Mookherji family for at least a dozen generations, helped along by shrewdly planned marriages designed to conserve the precious gene; he was more adept than any of his ancestors, yet it might take another century or two of Mookherjis to produce a really potent telepath. At least he was able to make good use of such talent for mind-contact as he had. He knew that many members of his family in earlier times had been forced to hide their gift from those about them, back in India, lest they be classed with vampires and werewolves and cast out of society.

Gently he placed his dark hand on Satina's pale wrist. Physical contact was necessary to attain the mental linkage. He concentrated on reaching her. After months of teletherapy, her mind was sensitized to his; he was able to skip the intermediate steps and, once he was warmed up, could plunge straight into her troubled soul. His eyes were closed. He saw a swirl of pearl-gray fog before him: Satina's mind. He thrust himself into it, entering easily. Up from the depths of her spirit swam a question mark.

—*Who is it? Doctor?*

—*Me, yes. How are you today, Satina?*

—*Fine. Just fine.*

—*Been sleeping well?*

—*It's so peaceful here, doctor.*

—*Yes. Yes, I imagine it is. But you ought to see how it is here. A wonderful summer day. The sun in the blue sky. Everything in bloom. A perfect day for swimming, eh? Wouldn't you like a swim?* He puts

all the force of his concentration into images of
swimming: a cold mountain stream, a deep pool
at the base of a creamy waterfall, the sudden delightful shock of diving in, the crystal flow tingling
against her warm skin, the laughter of her friends,
the splashing, the swift powerful strokes carrying her
to the far shore—

—*I'd rather stay where I am,* she tells him.

—*Maybe you'd like to go floating instead?* He summons the sensations of free flight: a floater-node fastened to her belt, lifting her serenely to an altitude of
a hundred feet, and off she goes, drifting over fields
and valleys, her friends beside her, her body totally
relaxed, weightless, soaring on the updrafts, rising until the ground is a checkerboard of brown and green,
looking down on the tiny houses and the comical cars,
now crossing a shimmering silvery lake, now hovering
over a dark, somber forest of thick-packed spruce, now
simply lying on her back, legs crossed, hands clasped
behind her head, the sunlight bright on her cheeks,
three hundred feet of nothingness underneath her—

But Satina doesn't take his bait. She prefers to stay
where she is. The temptations of floating are not
strong enough.

Mookherji does not have enough energy left to try
a third attempt at luring her out of her coma. Instead
he shifts to a purely medical function and tries to
probe for the source of the trauma that has cut her
off from the world. The fright, no doubt; and the terrible crack in the dome, spelling the end to all security;
and the sight of her parents and brother dying before

her eyes; and the swampy reek of Titan's atmosphere hitting her nostrils—all of those things, no doubt. But people have rebounded from worse calamities. Why does she insist on withdrawing from life? Why not come to terms with the dreadful past, and accept existence again?

But she fights him. Her defenses are fierce; she does not want him meddling with her mind. All of their sessions have ended this way: Satina clinging to her retreat, Satina blocking any shot at knocking her free of her self-imposed prison. He has gone on hoping that one day she will lower her guard. But this is not to be the day. Wearily, he pulls back from the core of her mind and talks to her on a shallower level.

—*You ought to be getting back to school, Satina.*

—*Not yet. It's been such a short vacation!*

—*Do you know how long?*

—*About three weeks, isn't it?*

—*Sixteen months so far,* he tells her.

—*That's impossible. We just went away to Titan a little while ago—the week before Christmas, wasn't it, and—*

—*Satina, how old are you?*

—*I'll be fifteen in April.*

—*Wrong,* he tells her. *That April's been here and gone, and so has the next one. You were sixteen two months ago. Sixteen, Satina.*

—*That can't be true, doctor. A girl's sixteenth birthday is something special, don't you know that? My parents are going to give me a big party. All my friends*

*invited. And a nine-piece robot orchestra with syn-
thesizers. And I know that that hasn't happened yet,
so how can I be sixteen?*

His reservoir of strength is almost drained. His mental signal is weak. He cannot find the energy to tell her
that she is blocking reality again, that her parents are
dead, that time is passing while she lies here, that it
is too late for a Sweet Sixteen party.

—*We'll talk about it . . . another time, Satina. I'll
. . . see . . . you . . . again . . . tomorrow . . . . Tomorrow . . . morning. . . .*

—*Don't go so soon, doctor!* But he can no longer
hold the contact, and lets it break.

Releasing her, Mookherji stood up, shaking his
head. A shame, he thought. A damned shame. He went
out of the room on trembling legs, and paused a moment in the hall, propping himself against a closed
door and mopping his sweaty forehead. He was getting
nowhere with Satina. After the initial encouraging
period of contact, he had failed entirely to lessen the
intensity of her coma. She had settled quite comfortably into her delusive world of withdrawal, and, telepathy or no, he could find no way to blast her loose.

He took a deep breath. Fighting back a growing
mood of bleak discouragement, he went toward the
next patient's room.

8.

The operation was going smoothly. Two dozen
third-year medical students occupied the observation

deck of the surgical gallery on the starport hospital's third floor, studying Dr. Hammond's expert technique by direct viewing and by simultaneous microamplified relay to their individual desk-screens. The patient, a brain-tumor victim in his late sixties, was visible only as a head and shoulders protruding from a life-support chamber. His scalp had been shaved; blue lines and dark-red dots were painted on it to indicate the inner contours of the skull, as previously determined by short-range sonar-bounces; the surgeon had finished the job of positioning the lasers that would excise the tumor. The hard part was over. Nothing remained except to bring the lasers to full power and send their fierce, precise bolts of light slicing into the patient's brain. Cranial surgery of this kind was entirely bloodless; there was no need to cut through skin and bone to expose the tumor, for the beams of the lasers, calibrated to a millionth of an inch, would penetrate through minute openings and, playing on the tumor from different sides, would destroy the malignant growth without harming a bit of the surrounding healthy brain tissue. Planning was everything in an operation like this. Once the exact outlines of the tumor were determined, and the surgical lasers were mounted at the correct angles, any intern could finish the job.

For Dr. Hammond it was a routine procedure. He had performed a hundred operations of this kind in the past year alone. He gave the signal; the warning light glowed on the laser rack; the students in the gallery leaned forth expectantly—

And, just as the lasers' glittering fire leaped toward the operating table, the face of the anesthetized patient contorted weirdly, as though some terrifying dream had come drifting up out of the depths of the man's drugged mind. His nostrils flared; his lips drew back; his eyes opened wide; he seemed to be trying to scream; he moved convulsively, twisting his head to one side. The lasers bit deep into the patient's left temple, far from the indicated zone of the tumor. The right side of his face began to sag, all muscles paralyzed. The medical students looked at each other in bewilderment. Dr. Hammond, stunned, retained enough presence of mind to kill the lasers with a quick swipe of his hand. Then, gripping the operating table with both hands in his agitation, he peered at the dials and meters that told him the details of the botched operation. The tumor remained intact; a vast sector of the patient's brain had been devastated. "Impossible," Hammond muttered. What could goad a patient under anesthesia into jumping around like that? "Impossible. Impossible." He strode to the end of the table and checked the readings on the life-support chamber. The question now was not whether the brain tumor would be successfully removed; the immediate question was whether the patient was going to survive.

9.

By four that afternoon Mookherji had finished most of his chores. He had seen every patient; he had brought his progress charts up to date; he had fed a prognosis digest to the master computer that was the starport hospital's control center; he had even found time for a gulped lunch. Ordinarily, now, he could take the next four hours off, going back to his spartan room in the residents' building at the edge of the starport complex for a nap, or dropping in at the recreation center to have a couple of rounds of floater-tennis, or looking in at the latest cube-show, or whatever. His next round of patient-visiting didn't begin until eight in the evening. But he couldn't relax: there was that business of the quarantined spacemen to worry about. Nakadai had been sending test outputs over since two o'clock, and now they were stacked deep in Mookherji's data terminal. Nothing had carried an *urgent* flag, so Mookherji had simply let the reports pile up; but now he felt he ought to have a look. He tapped the keys of the terminal, requesting printouts, and Nakadai's outputs began to slide from the slot.

Mookherji ruffled through the yellow sheets. Reflexes, synapse charge, degree of neural ionization, endocrine balances, visual response, respiratory & circulatory, cerebral molecular exchange, sensory percepts, EEG both enhanced and minimated. . . . No, nothing unusual here. It was plain from the tests that the six men who had been to Norton's Star were badly in need of a vacation—frayed nerves, blurred reflexes —but there was no indication of anything more serious than chronic loss of sleep. He couldn't detect signs of brain lesions, infection, nerve damage, or other organic disabilities.

Why the nightmares, then?

He tapped out the phone number of Nakadai's office. "Quarantine," a crisp voice said almost at once, and moments later Nakadai's lean, tawny face appeared on the screen. "Hello, Pete. I was just going to call you."

Mookherji said, "I didn't finish up until a little while ago. But I've been through the outputs you sent over. Lee, there's nothing here."

"As I thought."

"What about the men? You were supposed to call me if any of them went into nightmares."

"None of them have," Nakadai said. "Falkirk and Rodriguez have been sleeping since eleven. Like lambs. Schmidt and Carroll were allowed to conk out at half past one. Webster and Schiavone hit the cots at three. All six are still snoring away, sleeping like they haven't slept in years. I've got them loaded with equipment and everything's reading perfectly normal. You want me to shunt the data to you?"

"Why bother? If they aren't hallucinating, what'll I learn?"

"Does that mean you plan to skip the mind-probes tonight?"

"I don't know," Mookherji said, shrugging. "I suspect there's no point in it, but let's leave that part open. I'll be finishing my evening rounds about eleven, and if there's some reason to get into the heads of those spacemen then, I will." He frowned. "But look— didn't they say that each one of them went into the nightmares on *every single sleep-shift?*"

"Right."

"And here they are, sleeping outside the ship for the first time since the nightmares started, and none of them having any trouble at all. And no sign of possible hallucinogenic brain lesions. You know something, Lee? I'm starting to come around to a very silly hypothesis that those men proposed this morning."

"That the hallucinations were caused by some unseen alien being?" Nakadai asked.

"Something like that. Lee, what's the status of the ship they came in on?"

"It's been through all the routine purification checks, and now it's sitting in an isolation vector until we have some idea of what's going on."

"Would I be able to get aboard it?" Mookherji asked.

"I suppose so, yes, but—why—?"

"On the wild shot that something external caused those nightmares, and that that something may still be aboard the ship. And perhaps a low-level telepath like myself will be able to detect its presence. Can you set up clearance fast?"

"Within ten minutes," Nakadai said. "I'll pick you up."

Nakadai came by shortly in a rollerbuggy. As they headed out toward the landing field, he handed Mookherji a crumpled spacesuit and told him to put it on.

"What for?"

"You may want to breathe inside the ship. Right now it's full of vacuum—we decided it wasn't safe to leave it under atmosphere. Also it's still loaded with radiation from the decontamination process. Okay?"

Mookherji struggled into the suit.

They reached the ship: a standard interstellar null-gravity-drive job, looking small and lonely in its corner of the field. A robot cordon kept it under isolation, but, tipped off by the control center, the robots let the two doctors pass. Nakadai remained outside; Mookherji crawled into the safety pouch and, after the hatch had gone through its admission cycle, entered the ship. He moved cautiously from cabin to cabin, like a man walking in a forest that was said to have a jaguar in every tree. While looking about, he brought himself as quickly as possible up to full telepathic receptivity, and, wide open, awaited telepathic contact with anything that might be lurking in the ship.

—*Go on. Do your worst.*

Complete silence on all mental wavelengths. Mookherji prowled everywhere: the cargo hold, the crew cabins, the drive compartment. Everything empty, everything still. Surely he would have been able to detect the presence of a telepathic creature in here, no matter how alien; if it was capable of reaching the mind of a sleeping spaceman, it could reach the mind of a waking telepath as well. After fifteen minutes he left the ship, satisfied.

"Nothing there," he told Nakadai. "We're still nowhere."

10.

The Vsiir was growing desperate. It had been roaming this building all day; judging by the quality of the solar radiation coming through the windows, night was beginning to fall now. And, though there were open minds on every level of the structure, the Vsiir had had no luck in making contact. At least there had been no more terminations. But it was the same story here as on the ship: whenever the Vsiir touched a human mind, the reaction was so negative as to make communication impossible. And yet the Vsiir went on and on and on, to mind after mind, unable to believe that this whole planet did not hold a single human to whom it could tell its story. It hoped it was not doing severe damage to these minds it was approaching; but it had its own fate to consider.

Perhaps this mind would be the one. The Vsiir started once more to tell its tale—

11.

Half past nine at night. Dr. Peter Mookherji, blood-shot, tense, hauled himself through his neuropathological responsibilities. The ward was full: a schizoid collapse, a catatonic freeze, Satina in her coma, half a dozen routine hysterias, a couple of paralysis cases, an aphasic, and plenty more, enough to keep him going for sixteen hours a day and strain his telepathic powers, not to mention his conventional medical skills, to their limits. Someday the ordeal of residency would be over; someday he'd be quit of this hospital, and would set up private practice on some sweet tropical isle, and commute to Bombay on week-ends to see his family, and spend his holidays on planets of distant stars, like any prosperous medical specialist. . . . Someday. He tried to banish such lavish fantasies from his mind. If you're going to look forward to anything, he told himself, look forward to midnight. To sleep. Beautiful, beautiful sleep. And then in the morning it all begins again, Satina and the coma, the schizoid, the catatonic, the aphasic . . .

As he stepped into the hall, going from patient to patient, his annunciator said, "Dr. Mookherji, please report at once to Dr. Bailey's office."

Bailey? The head of the neuropathology department, still hitting the desk this late? What now? But of course there was no ignoring such a summons. Mookherji notified the control center that he had been called off his rounds, and made his way quickly down the corridor to the frosted-glass door marked SAMUEL F. BAILEY, M.D.

He found at least half the neuropath staff there already: four of the other senior residents, most of the interns, even a few of the high-level doctors. Bailey, a puffy-faced, sandy-haired, fiftyish man of formidable professional standing, was thumbing a sheaf of outputs and scowling. He gave Mookherji a faint nod by way of greeting. They were not on the best of terms; Bailey, somewhat old-school in his attitudes, had not made a good adjustment to the advent of telepathy as a tool in the treatment of mental disturbance. "As I was just saying," Bailey began, "these reports have been accumulating all day, and they've all been dumped on me, God knows why. Listen: two cardiac patients under sedation undergo sudden violent shocks, described by one doctor as sensory overloads. One reacts with cardiac arrest, the other with cerebral hemorrhage. Both die. A patient being treated for endocrine restabilization develops a runaway adrenalin flow while asleep, and gets a six-month setback. A patient undergoing brain surgery starts jumping around on the operating table, despite adequate anesthesia, and gets badly carved up by the lasers. Et cetera. Serious problems like this all over the hospital today. Computer check of general EEG patterns show that fourteen patients, other than those mentioned, have experienced exceptionally severe episodes of nightmare in the last eleven hours, nearly all of them of such impact that the patient has sustained some degree of psychic damage and often actual physiological harm. Control center reports no case histories of previous epidemics of bad dreams. No reason to suspect a widespread dietary imbalance or similar cause for the outbreak. Nevertheless, sleeping patients are continuing to suffer, and those whose condition is particularly critical may be exposed to grave risks. Effective immediately, sedation of critical patients has been interrupted where feasible, and sleep schedules of other patients have been rearranged, but this is obviously not an expedient that is going to do much good if this outbreak continues into tomorrow." Bailey paused, glanced around the room, let his gaze rest on Mookherji. "Control center has offered one hypothesis: that a psychopathic individual with strong telepathic powers is at large in the hospital, preying on sleeping patients and transmitting images to them that take the form of horrifying nightmares. Mookherji, what do you make of that idea?"

Mookherji said, "It's perfectly feasible, I suppose, although I can't imagine why any telepath would want to go around distributing nightmares. But has control center correlated any of this with the business over at the quarantine building?"

Bailey stared at his output slips. "What business is that?"

"Six spacemen who came in early this morning, reporting that they'd all suffered chronic nightmares on their voyage homeward. Dr. Lee Nakadai's been testing them; he called me in as a consultant, but I couldn't discover anything useful. I imagine there are some late reports from Nakadai in my office, but—"

Bailey said, "Control center seems only to be concerned about events in the hospital, not in the starport complex as a whole. And if your six spacemen had their nightmares during their voyage, there's no chance that their symptoms are going to find their way onto—"

"That's just it!" Mookherji cut in. "They had their nightmares in space. But they've been asleep since morning, and Nakadai says they're resting peacefully. Meanwhile an outbreak of hallucinations has started over here. Which means that whatever was bothering them during their voyage has somehow got loose in the hospital today—some sort of entity capable of stirring up such dreams that they bring veteran spacemen to the edge of nervous breakdowns and can seriously injure or even kill someone in poor health." He realized that Bailey was looking at him strangely, and that Bailey was not the only one. In a more restrained tone, Mookherji said, "I'm sorry if this sounds fantastic to you. I've been checking it out all day, so I've had some time to get used to the concept. And things began to fit together for me just now. I'm not saying that my idea is necessarily correct. I'm simply saying that it's a reasonable notion, that it links up with the spacemen's own idea of what was bothering them, that it corresponds to the shape of the situation—and that it deserves a decent investigation if we're going to stop this stuff before we lose some more patients."

"All right, doctor," Bailey said. "How do you propose to conduct the investigation?"

Mookherji was shaken by that. He had been on the go all day; he was ready to fold. Here was Bailey abruptly putting him in charge of this snark-hunt, without even asking! But he saw there was no way to refuse. He was the only telepath on the staff. And, if the supposed creature really was at large in the hospital, how could it be tracked except by a telepath?

Fighting back his fatigue, Mookherji said rigidly, "Well, I'd want a chart of all the nightmare cases,

to begin with, a chart showing the location of
each victim and the approximate time of onset of
hallucination—"

12.

They would be preparing for the Festival of Changing now, the grand climax of the winter. Thousands
of Vsiirs in the metamorphic phase would be on their
way toward the Valley of Sand, toward that great natural amphitheater where the holiest rituals were performed. By now the firstcomers would already have
taken up their positions, facing the west, waiting for
the sunrise. Gradually the rows would fill as Vsiirs
came in from every part of the planet, until the golden
valley was thick with them, Vsiirs that constantly
shifted their energy-levels, dimensional extensions,
and inner resonances, shuttling gloriously through the
final joyous moments of the season of metamorphosis,
competing with one another in a gentle way to display
the greatest variety of form, the most dynamic cycle
of physical changes—and, as the first red rays of the
sun crept past the Needle, the celebrants would grow
even more frenzied, dancing and leaping and trans-
forming themselves with total abandon, purging themselves of the winter's flamboyance as the season of
stability swept across the world. And finally, in the
full blaze of sunlight, they would turn to one another
in renewed kinship, embracing, and—

The Vsiir tried not to think about it. But it was hard to repress that sense of loss, that pang of nostalgia. The pain grew more intense with every moment. No imaginable miracle would get the Vsiir home in time for the Festival of Changing, it knew, and yet it could not really believe that such a calamity had befallen it.

Trying to touch minds with humans was useless. Perhaps if it assumed a form visible to them, and let itself be noticed, and *then* tried to open verbal communication—

But the Vsiir was so small, and these humans were so large. The dangers were great. The Vsiir, clinging to a wall and carefully keeping its wavelength well beyond the ultraviolet, weighed one risk against another, and, for the moment, did nothing.

13.

"All right," Mookherji said foggily, a little before midnight. "I think we've got the trail clear now." He sat before a wall-sized screen on which the control center had thrown a three-dimensional schematic plan of the hospital. Bright red dots marked the place of each nightmare incident, yellow dashes the probable path of the unseen alien creature. "It came in the side way, probably, straight off the ship, and went into the cardiac wing first. Mrs. Maldonado's bed here, Mr. Guinness' over here, eh? Then it went up to the second level, coming around to the front wing and impinging on the minds of patients here and here and here between ten and eleven in the morning. There were no reported episodes of hallucination in the next hour and ten minutes, but then came that nasty business in the third-level surgical gallery, and after that—" Mookherji's aching eyes closed a moment; it seemed to him that he could still see the red dots and yellow dashes. He forced himself to go on, tracing the rest of the intruder's route for his audience of doctors and hospital security personnel. At last he said, "That's it. I figure that the thing must be somewhere between the fifth and eighth levels by now. It's moving much more slowly than it did this morning, possibly running out of energy. What we have to do is keep the hospital's wing tightly sealed to prevent its free movement, if that can be done, and attempt to narrow down the number of places where it might be found."

One of the security men said, a little belligerently, "Doctor, just how are we supposed to find an invisible entity?"

Mookherji struggled to keep impatience out of his voice. "The visible spectrum isn't the only sort of electromagnetic energy in the universe. If this thing is alive, it's got to be radiating *somewhere* along the line. You've got a master computer with a million sensory pickups mounted all over the hospital. Can't you have the sensors scan for a point-source of infrared or ultraviolet moving through a room? Or even X rays, for God's sake: we don't know where the radiation's likely to be. Maybe it's a gamma emitter, even. Look, something wild is loose in this building, and we can't see it, but the computer can. Make it search."

Dr. Bailey said, "Perhaps the energy we ought to be trying to trace it by is, ah, telepathic energy, doctor."

Mookherji shrugged. "As far as anybody knows, telepathic impulses propagate somewhere outside the electromagnetic spectrum. But of course you're right that I might be able to pick up some kind of output, and I intend to make a floor-by-floor search as soon as this briefing session is over." He turned toward Nakadai. "Lee, what's the word from your quarantined spacemen?"

"All six went through eight-hour sleep periods today without any sign of a nightmare episode: some dreaming, but all of it normal. In the past couple of hours I've had them on the phone talking with some of the patients who had the nightmares, and everybody agrees that the kind of dreams people have been having here today are the same in tone, texture, and general level of horror as the ones the men had aboard the ship. Images of bodily destruction and alien landscapes, accompanied by an overwhelming, almost intolerable, feeling of isolation, loneliness, separation from one's own kind."

"Which would fit the hypothesis of an alien being as the cause," said Martinson of the psychology staff. "If it's wandering around trying to communicate with us, trying to tell us it doesn't want to be here, say, and its communications reach human minds only in the form of frightful nightmares—"

"Why does it communicate only with sleeping people?" an intern asked.

"Perhaps those are the only ones it can reach. Maybe a mind that's awake isn't receptive," Martinson suggested.

"Seems to me," a security man said, "that we're making a whole lot of guesses based on no evidence at all. You're all sitting around talking about an invisible telepathic thing that breathes nightmares in people's ears, and it might just as easily be a virus that attacks the brain, or something in yesterday's food, or—"

Mookherji said, "The ideas you're offering now have already been examined and discarded. We're working on this line of inquiry now because it seems to hold together, fantastic though it sounds, and because it's all we have. If you'll excuse me, I'd like to start checking the building for telepathic output, now." He went out, pressing his hands to his throbbing temples.

14.

Satina Ransom stirred, stretched, subsided. She looked up and saw the dazzling blaze of Saturn's rings overhead, glowing through the hotel's domed roof. She had never seen anything more beautiful in her life. This close to them, only about 750,000 miles out, she could clearly make out the different zones of the rings, each revolving about Saturn at its own speed, with the blackness of space visible through the open places. And Saturn itself, gleaming in the heavens, so bright, so huge—

What was that rumbling sound? Thunder? Not here, not on Titan. Again: louder. And the ground swaying. A crack in the dome! Oh, no, no, no, feel the air rushing out, look at that cold greenish mist pouring in—people falling down all over the place—what's happening, what's happening, what's happening? Saturn seems to be falling toward us. That taste in my mouth—oh—oh—oh—

Satina screamed. And screamed. And went on screaming as she slipped down into darkness, and pulled the soft blanket of unconsciousness over her, and shivered, and gave thanks for finding a safe place to hide.

15.

Mookherji had plodded through the whole building, accompanied by three security men and a couple of interns. He had seen whole sectors of the hospital that he didn't know existed. He had toured basements and sub-basements and sub-sub-basements; he had been through laboratories and computer rooms and wards and exercise chambers. He had kept himself in a state of complete telepathic receptivity throughout the trek, but he had detected nothing, not even a flicker of mental current anywhere. Somehow that came as no surprise to him. Now, with dawn near, he wanted nothing more than sixteen hours or so of sleep. Even with nightmares. He was tired beyond all comprehension of the meaning of tiredness.

Yet something wild was loose, still, and the nightmares still were going on. Three incidents, ninety minutes apart, had occurred during the night: two patients on the fifth level and one on the sixth had awakened in states of terror. It had been possible to calm them quickly, and apparently no lasting harm had been done; but now the stranger was close to Mookherji's neuropathology ward, and he didn't like the thought of exposing a bunch of mentally unstable patients to that kind of stimulus. By this time, the control center had reprogrammed all patient-monitoring systems to watch for the early stages of nightmare—hormone changes, EEG tremors, respiration-rate rise, and so forth—in the hope of awakening a victim before the full impact could be felt. Even so, Mookherji wanted to see that thing caught and out of the hospital before it got to any of his own people.

But how?

As he trudged back to his sixth-level office, he considered some of the ideas people had tossed around in that midnight briefing session. *Wandering around trying to communicate with us,* Martinson had said. *Its communications reach human minds only in the form of frightful nightmares. Maybe a mind's that's awake isn't receptive.* Even the mind of a human telepath, it seemed, wasn't receptive while awake. Mookherji wondered if he should go to sleep and hope the alien would reach him, and then try to deal with it, lead it into a trap of some kind—but no. He wasn't that different from other people. If he slept, and the alien did open contact, he'd simply have a hell of a nightmare and wake up, with nothing gained. That wasn't the answer. Suppose, though, he managed to make contact with the alien through the mind of a nightmare victim—someone he could use as a kind of telepathic loudspeaker, someone who wasn't likely to wake up while the dream was going on—

Satina.

Perhaps. Perhaps. Of course, he'd have to make sure the girl was shielded from possible harm. She had enough horrors running free in her head as it was. But if he lent her his strength, drained off the poison of the nightmare, took the impact himself via their telepathic link, and was able to stand the strain and still speak to the alien mind—that might just work. Might.

He went to her room. He clasped her hand between his.

—*Satina?*

—*Morning so soon, doctor?*

—*It's still early, Satina. But things are a little unusual here today. We need your help. You don't have to if you don't want to, but I think you can be of great*

*value to us, and maybe even to yourself. Listen to me
very carefully, and think it over before you say yes
or no—*

God help me if I'm wrong, Mookherji thought, far
below the level of telepathic transmission.

16.

Chilled, alone, growing groggy with dismay and
hopelessness, the Vsiir had made no attempts at contact for several hours now. What was the use? The
results were always the same when it touched a human mind; it was exhausting itself and apparently
bothering the humans, to no purpose. Now the sun
had risen. The Vsiir contemplated slipping out of the
building and exposing itself to the yellow solar radiation while dropping all defenses; it would be a quick
death, an end to all this misery and longing. It was
folly to dream of seeing the home planet again. And—
    What was that?
    A call. Clear, intelligible, unmistakable. *Come to
me.* An open mind somewhere on this level, speaking
neither the human language nor the Vsiir language,
but using the wordless, universally comprehensible
communion that occurs when mind speaks directly to
mind. *Come to me. Tell me everything. How can I
help you?*
    In its excitement the Vsiir slid up and down the

spectrum, emitting a blast of infrared, a jagged blurt of ultraviolet, a lively blaze of visible light, before getting control. Quickly it took a fix on the direction of the call. Not far away: down this corridor, under this door, through this passage. *Come to me.* Yes. Yes. Extending its mind-probes ahead of it, groping for contact with the beckoning mind, the Vsiir hastened forward.

17.

Mookherji, his mind locked to Satina's, felt the sudden crashing shock of the nightmare moving in, and even at second remove the effect was stunning in its power. He perceived a clicking sensation of mind touching mind. And then, into Satina's receptive spirit, there poured—

A wall higher than Everest. Satina trying to climb it, scrambling up a smooth white face, digging fingertips into minute crevices. Slipping back one yard for every two gained. Below, a roiling pit, flames shooting up, foul gases rising, monsters with needle-sharp fangs waiting for her to fall. The wall grows taller. The air is so thin—she can barely breathe, her eyes are dimming, a greasy hand is squeezing her heart, she can feel her veins pulling free of her flesh like wires coming out of a broken plaster ceiling, and the gravitational pull is growing constantly—pain, her lungs

crumbling, her face sagging hideously—a river of terror surging through her skull—

—*None of it is real, Satina. They're just illusions.
None of it is really happening.*

—*Yes,* she says, *yes, I know.* But still she resonates
with fright, her muscles jerking at random, her face
flushed and sweating, her eyes fluttering beneath the
lids. The dream continues. How much more can she
stand?

—*Give it to me,* he tells her. *Give me the dream!*

She does not understand. No matter. Mookherji
knows how to do it. He is so tired that fatigue is un-
important; somewhere in the realm beyond collapse
he finds unexpected strength, and reaches into her
numbed soul, and pulls the hallucinations forth as
though they were cobwebs. They engulf him. No
longer does he experience them indirectly; now all the
phantoms are loose in his skull, and, even as he feels
Satina relax, he braces himself against the onslaught
of unreality that he has summoned into himself. And
he copes. He drains the excess of irrationality out of
her and winds it about his consciousness, and adapts,
learning to live with the appalling flood of images.
He and Satina share what is coming forth. Together
they can bear the burden; he carries more of it than
she does, but she does her part, and now neither of
them is overwhelmed by the parade of bogeys. They
can laugh at the dream-monsters; they can even ad-
mire them for being so richly fantastic. That beast
with a hundred heads, that bundle of living copper

wires, that pit of dragons, that coiling mass of spiky teeth—who can fear what does not exist?

Over the clatter of bizarre images Mookherji sends a coherent thought, pushing it through Satina's mind:

—*Can you turn off the nightmares?*

—*No*, something replies. *They are in you, not in me. I only provide the liberating stimulus. You generate the images.*

—*All right. Who are you, and what do you want here?*

—*I am a Vsiir.*

—*A what?*

—*Native life-form of the planet where you collect the greenfire branches. Through my own carelessness I was transported to your planet.* Accompanying the message is an overriding impulse of sadness, a mixture of pathos, self-pity, discomfort, exhaustion. Above this the nightmares still flow, but they are insignificant now. The Vsiir says, *I wish only to be sent home. I did not want to come here.*

And this is our alien monster? Mookherji thinks. This is our fearsome, nightmare-spreading beast from the stars?

—*Why do you spread hallucinations?*

—*This was not my intention. I was merely trying to make mental contact. Some defect in the human receptive system, perhaps—I do not know. I do not know. I am so tired, though. Can you help me?*

—*We'll send you home, yes*, Mookherji promises. *Where are you? Can you show yourself to me? Let me know how to find you, and I'll notify the starport authorities, and they'll arrange for your passage home on the first ship out.*

Hesitation. Silence. Contact wavers and perhaps breaks.

—*Well?* Mookherji says, after a moment. *What's happening? Where are you?*

From the Vsiir an uneasy response:

—*How can I trust you? Perhaps you merely wish to destroy me. If I reveal myself—*

Mookherji bites his lip in sudden fury. His reserve of strength is almost gone; he can barely sustain the contact at all. And if he now has to find some way of persuading a suspicious alien to surrender itself, he may run out of steam before he can settle things. The situation calls for desperate measures.

—*Listen, Vsiir. I'm not strong enough to talk much longer, and neither is this girl I'm using. I invite you into my head. I'll drop all defenses: if you can look at who I am, look hard, and decide for yourself whether you can trust me. After that it's up to you. I can help you get home, but only if you produce yourself right away.*

He opens his mind wide. He stands mentally naked.

The Vsiir rushes into Mookherji's brain.

18.

A hand touched Mookherji's shoulder. He snapped awake instantly, blinking, trying to get his bearings.

Lee Nakadai stood above him. They were in—where?
—Satina Ransom's room. The pale light of early morning was coming through the window; he must have
dozed only a minute or so. His head was splitting.

"We've been looking all over for you, Pete," Nakadai
said.

"It's all right now," Mookherji murmured. "It's all
all right." He shook his head to clear it. He remembered things. Yes. On the floor, next to Satina's
bed, squatted something about the size of a frog, but
very different in shape, color, and texture from any
frog Mookherji had ever seen. He showed it to Nakadai. "That's the Vsiir," Mookherji said. "The alien
terror. Satina and I made friends with it. We talked it
into showing itself. Listen, it isn't happy here, so will
you get hold of a starport official fast, and explain
that we've got an organism here that has to be
shipped back to Norton's Star at once, and—"

Satina said, "Are you Dr. Mookherji?"

"That's right. I suppose I should have introduced
myself when—*you're awake?*"

"It's morning, isn't it?" The girl sat up, grinning.
"You're younger than I thought you were. And so
serious-looking. And I *love* that color of skin. I—"

"*You're awake?*"

"I had a bad dream," she said. "Or maybe a bad
dream within a bad dream—I don't know. Whatever it
was, it was pretty awful, but I felt so much better
when it went away—I just felt that if I slept any
longer I was going to miss a lot of good things, that I

had to get up and see what was happening in the world—do you understand any of this, doctor?"

Mookherji realized his knees were shaking. "Shock therapy," he muttered. "We blasted her loose from the coma—without even knowing what we were doing." He moved toward the bed. "Listen, Satina, I've been up for about a million years, and I'm ready to burn out from overload. And I've got a thousand things to talk about with you, only not now. Is that okay? Not now. I'll send Dr. Bailey in—he's my boss—and after I've had some sleep I'll come back and we'll go over everything together, okay? Say, five, six this evening. All right?"

"Well, of course, all right," Satina said, with a twinkling smile. "If you feel you really have to run off, just when I've—sure. Go. Go. You look awfully tired, doctor."

Mookherji blew her a kiss. Then, taking Nakadai by the elbow, he headed for the door. When he was outside he said, "Get the Vsiir over to your quarantine place pronto and try to put it in an atmosphere it finds comfortable. And arrange for its trip home. I'll go talk to Bailey—and then I'm going to drop."

Nakadai nodded. "You get some rest, Pete. I'll handle things."

Mookherji shuffled slowly down the hall toward Dr. Bailey's office, thinking of the smile on Satina's face, thinking of the sad little Vsiir, thinking of nightmares—

"Pleasant dreams, Pete," Nakadai called.

Riya's Foundling

BY ALGIS BUDRYS

Algis Budrys is male and his unusual name is of Lithuanian origin, to answer at once the two questions readers most frequently ask about him. He lives in the Chicago area, works at the public-relations trade when not writing science fiction, spends a lot of his time riding bicycles, and presides over a household full of (at the moment) adolescent and almost-adolescent sons. The story here is one of his earliest, published when he was barely out of his own adolescence: a moving, sensitive, and skillful portrait of a small boy with strange powers and his large otherworldly foster mother.

The loft of the feed-house, with its stacked grainsacks, was a B-72, a fort, a foxhole—any number of things, depending on Phildee's moods.

Today it was a jumping-off place.

Phildee slipped out of his dormitory and ran across the yard to the feed-house. He dropped the big wooden latch behind him and climbed up the ladder to the loft, depending on the slight strength of his young arms more than on his legs, which had to be lifted to straining heights before they could negotiate the man-sized rungs.

He reached the loft and stood panting, looking out over the farm through the loft door, at the light wooden fences around it, and the circling antenna of the radar tower.

Usually, he spent at least a little time each day crouched behind the grain-sacks and being bigger and older, firing coolly and accurately into charging companies of burly, thick-lipped UES soldiers, or going over on one wing and whistling down on a flight of TT-34's that scattered like frightened ducks before the fiery sleet of his wing rockets.

But today was different, today there was something he wanted to try.

He stood up on his toes and searched. He felt the touch of Miss Cowan's mind, no different from that of anyone else—flat, unsystematic.

He sighed. Perhaps, somewhere, there was someone else like himself. For a moment, the fright of loneliness invaded him, but then faded. He took a last

look at the farm, then moved away from the open
door, letting his mind slip into another way of
thinking.

His chubby features twisted into a scowl of concentration as he visualized reality. The scowl became
a deeper grimace as he negated that reality, step by
step, and substituted another.

F is for Phildee.

O is for Out.

R is for Reimann.

T is for Topology.

H is for heartsick hunger.

Abruptly, the Reimann fold became a concrete visualization. As though printed clearly in and around the
air, which was simultaneously both around him and
not around him, which existed/not existed in space-
time, he saw the sideslip diagram.

He twisted.

Spring had come to Riya's world; spring and the
thousand sounds of it. The melted snow in the moun-
taintops ran down in traceries of leaping water, and
the spring crests raced along the creeks into the rivers.
The riverbank grasses sprang into life; the plains
turned green again.

Riya made her way up the path across the foothills,
conscious of her shame. The green plain below her
was dotted, two by two, with the figures of her people.
It was spring, and Time. Only she was alone.

There was a special significance in the fact that she

was here on this path in this season. The plains on
either side of the brown river were her people's terri-
tory. During the summer, the couples ranged over the
grass until the dams were ready to drop their calves.
Then it became the bulls' duty to forage for their entire families until the youngsters were able to travel
south to the winter range.

Through the space of years, the people had increased in numbers, the pressure of this steady growth
making itself felt as the yearlings filled out on the winter range. It had become usual, as the slow drift
northward was made toward the end of winter, for
some of the people to split away from the main body
and range beyond the gray mountains that marked
the western limits of the old territories. Since these
wanderers were usually the most willful and head-
strong, they were regarded as quasi-outcasts by the
more settled people of the old range.

But—and here Riya felt the shame pierce more
strongly than ever—they had their uses, occasionally.
Preoccupied in her shame, she involuntarily turned
her head downward, anxious that none of the people
be staring derisively upward at the shaggy brown
hump of fur that was she, toiling up the path.

She was not the first—but that was meaningless.
That other female people had been ugly or old, that
the same unforgotten force that urged her up the
mountain path had brought others here before her,
meant only that she was incapable of accepting the
verdict of the years that had thinned her pelt, dimmed
her eyes, and broken the smooth rhythm of her gait.

In short, it meant that Riya Sair, granddam times over, spurned by every male on the old range, was willing to cross the gray mountains and risk death from the resentful wild dams for the thin hope that there was a male among the wildlings who would sire her calf.

She turned her head back to the path and hurried on, cringing in inward self-reproach at her speed.

Except for her age, Riya presented a perfect average of her people. She stood two yards high and two wide at the shoulders, a yard at the haunches, and measured three and a half yards from her muzzle to the rudimentary tail. Her legs were short and stumpy, cloven-hooved. Her massive head hung slightly lower than her shoulders, and could be lowered to within an inch or two of the ground. She was herbivorous, ruminant, and mammalian. Moreover, she had intelligence —not of a very high order, but adequate for her needs.

From a Terrestrial point of view, none of this was remarkable. Many years of evolution had gone into her fashioning—more years for her one species than for all the varieties of man that have ever been. Nevertheless, she did have some remarkable attributes.

It was one of these attributes that now enabled her to sense what happened on the path ahead of her. She stopped still, only her long fur moving in the breeze.

Phildee—five, towheaded, round faced, chubby, dressed in a slightly grubby corduroy oversuit, and precocious—had his attributes, too. Grubby and tousled; branded with a thread of licorice from one corner of his mouth to his chin; involved in the loss of his first milk-tooth, as he was—he nevertheless slipped onto the path on Riya's world, the highest product of Terrestrial evolution. Alice followed a white rabbit down a hole. Phildee followed Reimann down into a hole that, at the same time, followed him, and emerged—where?

Phildee didn't know. He could have performed the calculation necessary to the task almost instantly, but he was five. It was too much trouble.

He looked up, and saw a gray slope of rock vaulting above him. He looked down, and saw it fall away toward a plain on which were scattered pairs of foraging animals. He felt a warm breeze, smelled it, saw it blow dust along the path, and saw Riya:

B is for big brown beast.

L is for looming large, looking lonely.

B? L? Bull? No—bison.

Bison:

bison (bi'sn) *n.* The buf-
falo of the N. Amer. plains.

Phildee shook his head and scowled. No—not bison, either. What, then? He probed.

Riya took a step forward. The sight of a living organism other than a person was completely unfamiliar to her. Nevertheless, anything that small, and undeniably covered—in most areas, at least—with some kind of fur, could not, logically, be anything but a strange kind of calf. But—she stopped, and raised her head—if a calf, then where was the call?

Phildee's probe swept past the laboring mind directly into her telepathic, instinctual centers.

Voiceless, with their environment so favorable that it had never been necessary for them to develop prehensile limbs, female people had nevertheless evolved a method of child care commensurate with their comparatively higher intelligence.

Soft as tender fingers, gentle as the human hand that smooths the awry hair back from the young forehead, Riya's mental caress enfolded Phildee.

Phildee recoiled. The feeling was:

$$\left. \begin{array}{l} Warm \\ Soft \\ Sweet \end{array} \right\} \text{Not } candy \text{ in the mouth}$$

$$Candy \text{ in the mouth} \left\{ \begin{array}{l} Familiar \\ Good \\ Tasty \\ Nice \end{array} \right.$$

$$The \text{ } feeling \text{ } was \left\{ \begin{array}{l} Not \text{ } Familiar \\ Not \text{ } Good \\ Not \text{ } Tasty \\ Not \text{ } Nice \end{array} \right.$$

WHY?

M is for many motionless months.
T is for tense temper tantrums.
R is for rabid—NO!—rapid rolling wrench.

MTR. Mother.

Phildee's mother wanted Phildee's father. Phildee's mother wanted green grass and apple trees, tight skirts and fur jackets on Fifth Avenue, men to turn and look, a little room where nobody could see her. Phildee's mother had radiation burns. Phildee's mother was dead.

He wavered; physically. Maintaining his position in this world was a process that demanded constant attention from the segment of his mind devoted to it. For a moment, even that small group of brain cells almost became involved in his reaction.

It was that which snapped him back into functioning logically. MTR was Mother. Mother was:

Tall
Thin   }   *"In Heaven's name, Doctor,*
White   *when will this thing be over?"*
Biped

BL was Riya. Riya was:
Big brown beast, looming large, looking lonely.
BL=MTR
Equation not meaningful, not valid.

Almost resolved, only a few traces of the initial conflict remained. Phildee put the tips of his right fingers to his mouth. He dug his toe into the ground, gouged a semicircular furrow, and smoothed it over with his sole.

Riya continued to look at him from where she was standing, two or three feet away. Haltingly, she reached out her mind again—hesitating not because of fear of another such reaction on Phildee's part, for that had been far beyond her capacity to understand, but because even the slightest rebuff on the part of a child to a gesture as instinctive as a Terrestrial mother's caress was something that none of the people had ever encountered before.

While her left-behind intellectual capacity still struggled to reconcile the feel of childhood with a visual image of complete unfamiliarity, the warm mind-caress went gently forth again.

Phildee made up his mind. Ordinarily, he was immune to the small emotional problems that beclouded less rational intellects. He was unused to functioning in other than a cause/effect universe. Mothers were usually—though sometimes not—matronly women who spent the greater part of roughly twenty years per child in conscious preoccupation with, and/or subconscious or conscious rejection of, their offspring.

In his special case, Mother was a warm place, a frantic, hysteric voice, the pressure of the spasmodically contractile musculature linked to her hyperthyroid metabolism. Mother was a thing from before birth.

Riya—Riya bore a strong resemblance to an intelligent cow. In any physiological sense, she could no more be his mother than—

The second caress found him not unaccustomed to it. It enfolded his consciousness, tenderly, protectingly, empathetic.

Phildee gave way to instinct.

The fur along the ridge of Riya's spine prickled with a well-remembered happiness as she felt the hesitant answering surge in Phildee's mind. Moving surely forward, she nuzzled his face. Phildee grinned. He ran his fingers through the thick fur at the base of her short neck.

Big warm wall of brown fur.

Cool, happy nose.

Happy, happy eyes.

Great joy welled up in Riya. No shameful trot across the mountains faced her now. No hesitant approach to the huddled, suspicious wildlings was before her. The danger of sharp female hooves to be avoided, of skulking at the edge of the herd in hope of an anxious male, was a thing no longer to be half-fearfully approached.

With a nudge of her head, she directed Phildee down the path to the old range while she herself turned around. She stood motionless for a sweeping scan of the plain below her. The couples were scattered over the grass—but couples only, the females as yet unfulfilled.

This, too, was another joy to add to the greatest of all. So many things about her calf were incomprehensible—the only dimly felt overtones of projected symbology that accompanied Phildee's emotional reactions, the alien structure—so many, many things. Her mind floundered vainly through the complex data.

But all that was nothing. What did it matter? The Time had been, and for another season, she was a dam.

Phildee walked beside her down the path, one fist wrapped in the fur of her flank, short legs windmilling.

They reached the plain, and Riya struck out across it toward the greatest concentration of people, her head proudly raised. She stopped once, and deliberately cropped a mouthful of grass with unconcern, but resumed her pace immediately thereafter.

With the same unconcern, she nudged Phildee into the center of the group of people, and, ignoring them, began teaching her calf to feed.

Eat. (Picture of Phildee/calf on all fours, cropping the plains grass.)

Phildee stared at her in puzzlement. Grass was not food. He sent the data emphatically.

Riya felt the tenuous discontent. She replied with tender understanding. Sometimes the calf was hesitant.

Eat. (Gently, understandingly, but firmly. [Repetition of picture.]) She bent her head and pushed him carefully over, then held his head down with a gentle pressure of her muzzle. *Eat.*

Phildee squirmed. He slipped out from under her nose and regained his feet. He looked at the other people, who were staring in puzzlement at Riya and himself.

He felt himself pushed forward again. *Eat.*

Abruptly, he realized the situation. In a culture of herbivores, what food could there be but herbiage? There would be milk, in time, but not for—he probed —months.

In probing, too, he found the visualization of his life with her ready at the surface of Riya's mind.

There was no shelter on the plain. His fur was all the shelter necessary.

But I don't have any fur.

In the fall, they would move to the southern range.

Walk? A thousand miles?

He would grow big and strong. In a year, he would be a sire himself.

His reaction was simple, and practiced. He adjusted his reality concept to Reimannian topology. Not actually, but subjectively, he felt himself beginning to slip Earthward.

Riya stiffened in alarm. The calf was straying. The knowledge was relayed from her mother-centers to the telepathic functions.

Stop. You cannot go there. You must be with your mother. You are not grown. Stop. Stay with me. I will protect you. I love you.

The universe shuddered. Phildee adjusted frantically. Cutting through the delicately maintained reality concept was a scrambling, jamming frequency of thought. In terror, he flung himself backward into Riya's world. Standing completely still, he probed frantically into Riya's mind.

And found her mind only fumblingly beginning to intellectualize the simple formulization of what her instinctive centers had computed, systematized, and

activated before her conscious mind had even begun
to doubt that everything was well.

His mind accepted the data, and computed.

Handless and voiceless, not so fast afoot in their
bulkiness as the weakest month-old calf, the people
had long ago evolved the restraints necessary for rear-
ing their children.

If the calf romped and ran, his mother ran beside
him, and the calf was not permitted to run faster than
she. If a calf strayed from its sleeping mother, it
strayed only so far, and then the mother woke—but
the calf had already long been held back by the time
her intelligence awoke to the straying.

The knowledge and computations were fed in Phildee's rational centers. The Universe—and Earth—
were closed to him. He must remain here.

But human children could not survive in this
environment.

He had to find a solution—instantly.

He clinched his fists, feeling his arm muscles quiver.

His lower lip was pulled into his mouth, and his
teeth sank in.

The diagram—the pattern—bigger—stronger—try
—try—this is not real—*this* is real: brown earth,
white clouds, blue sky—try—mouth full of warm
salt. . .

F is for Phildee!
O is for Out!
R is for Riya!
T is for Topology!
H is for happiness and home!

Riya shook herself. She stood in the furrows of a plowed field, her eyes vacant with bewilderment. She stared uncomprehendingly at the walls and the radar tower, the concrete shoulders of the air raid bunkers. She saw antiaircraft quick-firers being hastily cranked around and down at her, heard Phildee's shout that saved her life, and understood none of it.

But none of it mattered. Her strange calf was with her, standing beside her with his fingers locked in her fur, and she could feel the warm response in his mind as she touched him with her caress again.

She saw the other little calves erupting out of the low dormitory buildings, and something within her crooned.

Riya nuzzled her foundling. She looked about her at the War Orphans' Relocation Farm with her happy, happy eyes.

Through Other Eyes

BY R. A. LAFFERTY

One of the most troublesome of philosophical questions is the one about how we know the world really is the way we see it. We all agree that pine needles are green and the sky is blue, but are the colors I think of as "green" and "blue" anything like the "green" and "blue" you see? Are there absolute shapes and forms, or is everything relative, is everything individual to the eye of the beholder? Perhaps if we had some sort of machine that allowed us to look through other eyes, we might feel more confident about the true nature of the world about us; and R. A. Lafferty gives us such a machine here.

197

I

"*I don't think* I can stand the dawn of another Great Day," said Smirnov. "It always seems a muggy morning, a rainy afternoon, and a dismal evening. You remember the Recapitulation Correlator?"

"Known popularly as the Time Machine. But, Gregory, that was and is a success. All three of them are in constant use, and they will construct at least one more a decade. They are invaluable."

"Yes. It was a dismal success. It has turned my whole life gray. You remember our trial run, the recapitulation of the Battle of Hastings?"

"It *was* a depressing three years we spent there. But how were we to know it was such a small affair—covering less than five acres of that damnable field and lasting less than twenty minutes? And how were we to know that an error of four years had been made in history even as recent as that? Yes, we scanned many depressing days and many muddy fields in that area before we recreated it."

"And our qualified success at catching the wit of Voltaire at first hand?"

"Gad! That cackle! There can never be anything new in nausea to one who has sickened of that. What a perverted old woman he was!"

"And Nell Guinn?"

"There is no accounting for the taste of a king. What a completely tasteless morsel!"

"And the crowning of Charlemagne?"

"The king of chilblains. If you wanted a fire, you

carried it with you in a basket. That was the coldest
Christmas I ever knew. But the mead seemed to
warm them; and we were the only ones present who
could not touch it or taste it."

"And when we went further back and heard the
wonderful words of the divine poetess Sappho."

"Yes, she had just decided that she would have her
favorite cat spayed. We listened to her for three days
and she talked of nothing else. How fortunate the
world is that so few of her words have survived."

"And watching the great Pythagoras at work."

"And the long days he spent on that little surveying
problem. How one longed to hand him a slide rule
through the barrier and explain its workings."

"And our eavesdropping on the great lovers Tristram
and Isolde."

"And him spending a whole afternoon trying to tune
that cursed harp with a penny whistle. And she could
talk of nothing but the bear grease she used on her
hair, and how it was nothing like the bear grease back
home. But she was a cute little lard barrel, quite the
cutest we found for several centuries in either direction. One wouldn't be able to get one's arms all the way
around her; but I can understand how, to one of that
era and region, it would be fun trying."

"Ah yes. Smelled like a cinnamon cookie, didn't she?
And you recall Lancelot?"

"Always had a bad back that wouldn't let him ride.
And that trick elbow and the old groin wound. He
spent more time on the rubbing table than any athlete
I ever heard of. If I had a high-priced quarterback who

was never ready to play, I'd sure find a way of breaking his contract. No use keeping him on the squad
just to read his ten-year-old press clippings. Any farm
boy could have pulled him off his nag and stomped
him into the dirt."

"I wasn't too happy about Aristotle the day we
caught him. That barbarous north-coast Greek of his!
Three hours he had them all busy curling his beard.
And his discourse on the *Beard in Essential* and the
Beard in Existential, did you follow that?"

"No, to tell the truth I didn't. I guess it was pretty
profound."

They were silent and sad for a while, as are men
who have lost much.

"The machine was a success," said Smirnov at last,
"and yet the high excitement of it died dismally for us."

"The excitement is in the discovery of the machine,"
said Cogsworth. "It is never in what the machine
discovers."

"And this new one of yours," said Smirnov, "I hardly
want to see you put it into operation. I am sure it will
be a shattering disappointment to you."

"I am sure of it also. And yet it is greater than the
other. I am as excited as a boy."

"You were a boy before, but you will never be again.
I should think it would have aged you enough, and I
cannot see what fascination this new one will have for
you. At least the other recaptured the past. This will
permit you to see only the present."

"Yes, but through other eyes."

"One pair of eyes is enough. I do not see any advantage at all except the novelty. I am afraid that this will be only a gadget."

"No. Believe me, Smirnov, it will be more than that. It may not even be the same world when viewed through different eyes. I believe that what we regard as one may actually be several billion different universes, each made only for the eyes of the one who sees it."

II

The Cerebral Scanner, newly completed by Charles Cogsworth, was not an intricate machine. It was a small but ingenious amplifying device, or battery of amplifiers, designed for the synchronous—perhaps "sympathetic" would be a better word—coupling of two very intricate machines: two human brains. It was an amplifier only. A subliminal coupling, or the possibility of it, was already assumed by the inventor. Less than a score of key aspects needed emphasizing for the whole thing to come to life.

Here the only concern was with the convoluted cortex of the brain itself, that house of consciousness and terminal of the senses, and with the quasi-electrical impulses which are the indicators of its activity. It had been a long-held opinion of Cogsworth that, by the proper amplification of a near score of these impulses in one brain, a transmission could be effected to another so completely that one man might for an instant see with the eyes of another—also see inwardly with that man's eyes, have the same imaginings and day-dreams, perceive the same universe as the other perceived. And it would not be the same universe as the seeking man knew.

The Scanner had been completed, as had a compilation of the dossiers of seven different brains: a collection of intricate brain-wave data as to frequency, impulse, flux and field, and Lyall-wave patterns of the seven cerebrums which Cogsworth would try to couple with his own.

The seven were those of Gregory Smirnov, his colleague and counselor in so many things; of Gaetan Balbo, the cosmopolitan and supra-national head of the Institute; of Theodore Grammont, the theoretical mathematician; of E. E. Euler, the many-tentacled executive; of Karl Kleber, the extraordinary psychologist; of Edmond Guillames, the skeptic and bloodless critic; and of Valery Mok, a lady of beauty and charm whom Cogsworth had despaired of ever understanding by ordinary means.

This idea of his—to enter into the mind of another, to peer from behind another's eyes into a world that could not be the same—this idea had been with him all his life. He recalled how it had first come down on him in all its strength when he was quite small.

"It may be that I am the only one who sees the sky black at night and the stars white," he had said to himself, "and everybody else sees the sky white and the stars shining black. And I say the sky is black, and they say the sky is black; but when they say black they mean white."

Or: "I may be the only one who can see the outside of a cow, and everybody else sees it inside out. And I say that it is the outside, and they say that it is the outside; but when they say outside they mean inside."

Or: "It may be that all the boys I see look like girls to everyone else, and all the girls look like boys. And I say 'That is a girl,' and they say 'That is a girl'; only when they say a girl they mean a boy."

And then had come the terrifying thought: "What if I am a girl to everyone except me?"

This did not seem very intelligent to him even when he was small, and yet it became an obsession to him.

"What if to a dog all dogs look like men and all men look like dogs? And what if a dog looks at me and thinks that I am a dog and he is a boy?"

And this was followed once by the shattering afterthought: "And what if the dog is right?

"What if a fish looks up at a bird and a bird looks down at a fish? And the fish thinks that he is the bird and the bird is the fish, and that he is looking down on the bird that is really a fish, and the air is water and the water is air?

"What if, when a bird eats a worm, the worm thinks he is the bird and the bird is the worm? And that his outside is his inside, and that the bird's inside is his outside? And that he has eaten the bird instead of the bird eating him?"

This was illogical. But how does one know that a worm is not illogical? He has much to make him illogical.

And as he grew older Charles Cogsworth came on many signs that the world he saw was not the world that others saw. There came smaller but persistent signs that every person lives in a different world.

It was early in the afternoon, but Charles Cogsworth sat in darkness. Gregory Smirnov had gone for a walk in the country as he said he would. He was the only other one who knew that the experiment was being made. He is the only one who would have agreed to the experiment, though the others had permitted their brain-wave dossiers to be compiled on another pretext.

All beginnings come quietly, and this one was a total success. The sensation of seeing with the eyes of another is new and glorious, though the full recognition of it comes slowly.

"He is a greater man than I," said Cogsworth. "I have often suspected it. He has a placidity which I do not own, though he has not my fever. And he lives in a better world."

It was a better world, greater in scope and more exciting in detail.

"Who would have thought of giving such a color to grass, if it is grass? It is what he calls grass, but it is not what I call grass. I wonder I should ever be content to see it as I saw it. It is a finer sky than I had known, and more structured hills. The old bones of them stand out for him as they do not for me, and he knows the water in their veins.

"There is a man walking toward him, and he is a grander man than I have ever seen. Yet I have also known the shadow of this man, and his name is Mr. Dottle, both to myself and to Gregory. I had thought that Dottle was a fool, but now I know that in the world of Gregory no man is a fool. I am looking through the inspired and almost divine eyes of a giant, and I am looking at a world that has not yet grown tired."

For what seemed like hours Charles Cogsworth lived in the world of Gregory Smirnov; and he found here, out of all his life, one great expectation that did not fail him.

Then, after he had rested a while, he looked at the world through the wide eyes of Gaetan Balbo.

"I am not sure that he is a greater man than I, but he is a wider man. Nor am I sure that he looks into a greater world. I would not willingly trade for his, as I would for Gregory's. Here I miss the intensity of my own. But it is fascinating, and I will enjoy returning to it again and again. And I know whose eyes these are. I am looking through the eyes of a king."

Later he saw through the eyes of Theodore Grammont, and felt a surge of pity.

"If I am blind compared to Gregory, then this man is blind compared to me. I at least know that the hills are alive; he believes them to be imperfect polyhedrons. He is in the middle of a desert and is not even able to talk to the devils who live there. He has abstracted the world and numbered it, and doesn't even know that the world is a live animal. He has built his own world of great complexity, but he cannot see the color of its flanks. This man has achieved so much only because he was denied so much at the beginning. I understand now that only the finest theory is no more than a fact gnawed on vicariously by one who has no teeth. But I will return to this world too, even though it has no body to it. I have been seeing through the eyes of a blind hermit."

Delightful and exciting as this was, yet it was tiring. Cogsworth rested for a quarter of an hour before he entered the world of E. E. Euler. When he entered it he was filled with admiration.

"An ordinary man could not look into a world like this. It would drive him out of his wits. It is almost like looking through the eyes of the Lord, who numbers all the feathers of the sparrow and every mite that nestles there. It is the interconnection vision of all the details. It appalls. It isn't an easy world even to look at. Great Mother of Ulcers! How does he stand it? Yet I see that he loves every tangled detail, the more tangled the better. This is a world in which I will be able to take only a clinical interest. Somebody must hold these reins, but happily it is not my fate. To tame this hairy old beast we live on is the doom of Euler. I look for a happier doom."

He had been looking through the eyes of a general.

The attempt to see into the world of Karl Kleber was almost total failure. The story is told of the behaviorist who would study the chimpanzee. He put the curious animal in a room alone and locked the door on it; then went to the keyhole to spy; the keyhole was completely occupied by the brown eyeball of the animal spying back at him.

Something of the sort happened here. Though Karl Kleber was unaware of the experiment, yet the seeing was in both directions. Kleber was studying Cogsworth in those moments by some quirk of circumstance. And even when Cogsworth was able to see with the eyes of Kleber, yet it was himself he was seeing.

"I am looking through the eyes of a peeper," he said. "And yet, what am I myself?"

If the world of Gregory Smirnov, first entered, was the grandest, so that of Edmond Guillames, which Cogsworth entered last but one, was in all ways the meanest. It was a world seen from the inside of a bile duct. It was not a pleasant world, just as Edmond was not a pleasant man. But how could one be other than a skeptic if all his life he had seen nothing but a world of rubbery bones and bloodless flesh clothed in crippled colors and obscene forms?

"The mole of another's world would be nobler than a lion in his," said Cogsworth. "Why should one not be a critic who has so much to criticize? Why should one not be an unbeliever when faced with the dilemma that this unsavory world was either made by God or hatched by a cross-eyed ostrich? I have looked through the eyes of a fool into a fools' world."

As Cogsworth rested again he said, "I have seen the

world through the eyes of a giant, of a king, of a blind hermit, of a general, of a peeping tom, of a fool. There is nothing left but to see it through the eyes of an angel."

Valery Mok may or may not have been an angel. She was a beautiful woman, and angels, in the older and more authentic iconography, were rather stern men with shaggy pinions.

Valery wore a look of eternal amusement, and was the embodiment of all charm and delight, at least to Charles Cogsworth. He believed her to be of high wit. Yet, if driven into a corner, he would have been unable to recall one witty thing she had ever said. He regarded her as of perfect kindness, and she *was* more or less on the agreeable side. Yet, as Smirnov had put it, she was not ordinarily regarded as extraordinary.

It was only quite lately that Cogsworth was sure that it was love he felt for her rather than bafflement. And, as he had despaired of ever understanding her by regular means, though everyone else understood her easily enough in as much as mattered, he would now use irregular means for his understanding.

He looked at the world through the eyes of Valery Mok, saying, "I will see the world through the eyes of an angel."

A change came over him as he looked, and it was not a pleasant change. He looked through her eyes quite a while—not, perhaps, as long as he had looked through the eyes of Gregory—yet for a long time, unable to tear himself away.

He shuddered and trembled and shrank back into himself.

Then he let it alone, and buried his face in his arms.

"I have looked at the world through the eyes of a pig," he said.

III

Charles Cogsworth spent six weeks in a sanatorium, which, however, was not called that. He had given the world his second great invention, and its completion had totally exhausted him. As in many such mercurial temperaments, the exaltation of discovery had been followed by an interlude of deep despondency on its completion.

Yet he was of fundamentally sound constitution and he had the best of care. But when he recovered it was not into his old self. He now had a sort of irony and smiling resignation that was new to him. It was as though he had discovered a new and more bitter world for himself in looking into the worlds of others.

Of his old intimates only Gregory Smirnov was still close to him.

"I can guess the trouble, Charles," said Gregory. "I rather feared this would happen. In fact I advised against her being one of the subjects of the experiment. It is simply that you know very little about women."

"I have read all the prescribed texts, Gregory. I took

a six-week seminar under Zamenoff. I am acquainted with almost the entire body of the work of Bopp concerning women. I have spent nearly as many years as you in the world, and I generally go about with my eyes open. I surely understand as much as is understandable about them."

"No. They are not your proper field. I could have predicted what has shocked you. You had not understood that women are so much more sensuous than men. But it would be better if you explained just what it was that shocked you."

"I had thought that Valery was an angel. It is simply that it was a shock to find that she is a pig."

"I doubt if you understand pigs any better than you understand women. I myself, only two days ago, had a pig's-eye view of the world, and that with your own Cerebral Scanner. I have been doing considerable work with it in the several weeks that you have been laid up. There is nothing in the pig's-eye world that would shock even the most fastidious. It is a dreamy world of all-encompassing placidity, almost entirely divorced from passion. It's a gray shadowy world with very little of the unpleasant. I had never before known how wonderful is the feel of simple sunlight and of cool earth. Yet we would soon be bored with it; but the pig is not bored."

"You divert me, Gregory, but you do not touch the point of my shock. Valery is beautiful—or was to me before this. She seemed kind and serene. Always she appeared to contain a mystery that amused her vastly, and which I suspected would be the most wonderful thing in the world once I understood it."

"And her mystery is that she lives in a highly sensuous world and enjoys it with complete awareness? Is that what has shocked you?"

"You do not know the depth of it. It is ghastly. The colors of that world are of unbelievable coarseness, and the shapes reek. The smells are the worst. Do you know how a tree smells to her?"

"What kind of tree?"

"Any tree. I think it was an ordinary elm."

"The Slippery Elm has a pleasant aroma in season. The others, to me, have none."

"No. It was not. Every tree has a strong smell in her world. This was an ordinary elm tree, and it had a violent musky obscene smell that delighted her. It was so strong that it staggered. And to her the grass itself is like clumps of snakes, and the world itself is flesh. Every bush is to her a leering satyr, and she cannot help but brush into them. The rocks are spidery monsters and she loves them. She sees every cloud as a mass of twisting bodies and she is crazy to be in the middle of them. She hugged a lamp post and her heart beat like it would fight its way out of her body.

"She can smell rain at a great distance and in a foul manner, and she wants to be in the middle of it. She worships every engine as a fire monster, and she hears sounds that I thought nobody could ever hear. Do you know what worms sound like inside the earth? They're devilish, and she would writhe and eat dirt with them.

She can rest her hand on a guard rail, and it is an obscene act when she does it. There is a filthiness in every color and sound and shape and smell and feel."

"And yet, Charles, she is but a slightly more than average attractive girl, given to musing, and with a love of the world and a closeness to it that most of us have lost. She has a keen awareness of reality and of the grotesqueness that is its main mark. You yourself do not have this deeply; and when you encounter it in its full strength, it shocks you."

"You mean this is normal?"

"There is no normal. There are only differences. When you moved into our several worlds they did not shock you to the same extent, for most of the corners are worn off our worlds. But to move into a pristine universe is more of a difference than you were prepared for."

"I cannot believe that that is all it is."

Charles Cogsworth would not answer the letters of Valery Mok, nor would he see her. Yet her letters were amusing and kind, and carried a trace of worry for him.

"I wonder what I smell like to her?" he asked himself. "Am I like an elm tree, or a worm in the ground? What color am I to her? Is my voice obscene? She says she misses the sound of my voice. It should be possible to undo this. Am I also to her like a column of snakes or a congeries of spiders?"

For he wasn't well yet from what he had seen.

But he did go back to work, and nibbled at the edges of mystery with his fantastic device. He even looked into the worlds of other women. It was as Smirnov had said: they were more sensuous than men but none of them to the shocking degree of Valery.

He saw with the eyes of other men. And of animals: the soft pleasure of the fox devouring a ground squirrel, the bloody anger of a lamb furious after milk, the crude arrogance of the horse, the intelligent tolerance of the mule, the voraciousness of the cow, the miserliness of the squirrel, the sullen passion of the catfish. Nothing was quite as might have been expected.

He learned the jealousy and hatred that beautiful women hold against the ugly, the untarnished evil of small children, the diabolic possession of adolescents. He even, by accident, saw the world through the fleshless eyes of a poltergeist, and through the eyes of creatures that he could not identify at all. He found nobility in places that almost balanced the pervading baseness.

But mostly he loved to see the world through the eyes of his friend Gregory Smirnov, for there was a grandeur on everything when seen through a giant's eyes.

And one day he saw Valery Mok through the eyes of Smirnov when they met accidentally. Something of his old feeling came back to him, and something that even surpassed his former regard. She was here magnificent, as was everything in that world. And there had to be a common ground between that wonderful world with her in it and the hideous world seen through her own eyes.

"I am wrong somewhere," said Cogsworth. "It is because I do not understand enough. I will go and see her."

But instead she came to see him.

She burst in on him furiously one day.

"You are a stick. You are a stick with no blood in it. You are a pig made out of sticks. You live with dead people, Charles. You make everything dead. You are abominable."

"I a pig, Valery? Possibly. But I never saw a pig made out of sticks."

"Then see yourself. That is what you are."

"Tell me what this is about."

"It is about you. You are a pig made out of sticks, Charles. Gregory Smirnov let me use your machine. I saw the world the way you see it. I saw it with a dead man's eyes. You don't even know that the grass is alive. You think it's only grass."

"I also saw the world with your eyes, Valery."

"Oh, is that what's been bothering you? Well, I hope it livened you up a little. It's a livelier world than yours."

"More pungent, at least."

"Lord, I should hope so. I don't think you even have a nose. I don't think you have any eyes. You can look at a hill and your heart doesn't even skip a beat. You don't even tingle when you walk over a field."

"You see grass like clumps of snakes."

"That's better than not even seeing it alive."

"You see rocks like big spiders."

"That's better than just seeing them like rocks. I love snakes and spiders. You can watch a bird fly by and not even hear the stuff gurgling in its stomach. How can you be so dead? And I always liked you so much. But I didn't know you were dead like that."

"How can one love snakes and spiders?"

"How can one love anything? It's even hard not to love you, even if you don't have any blood in you. By the way, what gave you the idea that blood was that dumb color? Don't you even know that blood is red?"

"I see it red."

"You *don't* see it red. You just call it red. That silly color isn't red. What I call red is red."

And he knew that she was right.

And after all, how can one not love anything? Especially when it becomes beautiful when angry, and when it is so much alive that it tends to shock by its intense awareness those who are partly dead.

Now Charles Cogsworth was a scientific man, and he believed that there are no insoluble problems. He solved this one too; for he had found that Valery was a low-flying bird, and he began to understand what was gurgling inside her.

And he solved it happily.

He is working on a Correlator for his Scanner now. When this is perfected, it will be safe to give the device to the public. You will be able to get the combination in about three years at approximately the price of a medium-sized new car. And if you will wait another year, you may be able to get one of the used ones reasonably.

The Correlator is designed to minimize and condition the initial view of the world seen through other eyes, to soften the shock of understanding others.

Misunderstandings can be agreeable. But there is something shattering about sudden perfect understanding.

The Conspirators

BY JAMES WHITE

James White lives in Northern Ireland, speaks with a lovely and curiously contagious lilting accent, and since the 1950's has quietly been producing some of the most thoughtful and intelligent science fiction published anywhere. Even at the outset of his career he was a capable craftsman, as this 1954 story of telepathic shenanigans aboard an interstellar spaceship amply demonstrates.

Something *had* gone wrong. It was outside his range, but Felix caught a sharp, incoherent sensation of mingled shock, loss, and panic in the instant that it happened. He floated, outwardly unconcerned, in the middle of the corridor which led to the Biology Section, and waited for the details to come down the line.

217

A few minutes later the relay who was clinging to the wall-net at the end of the corridor began sending him the facts. The news was very bad.

It seemed that the Small One whose job it was to damage certain tiny but important circuits in the Communications Room for purposes connected with the Escape had had an accident. Singer had seen it happen—Felix had guessed it was Singer. Even on the fourth leg of a relay the thought pattern was unmistakable; all emotion and not enough fact—the Small One had jumped for cover when he heard the crew-man coming, misjudged, and landed on a live section. It was only a couple of hundred volts, but that was an awful lot to a Small One—he was very thoroughly dead. What was left of him was floating in plain sight, and Singer was rapidly killing himself with his frenzied attempts at holding the crew-man's attention, because if the man noticed the body, and the disconnected wiring beside it, he might be suspicious. Singer wanted somebody to do something, *quick*. The message ended with a sense-free garble of fear, urgency and panic that was almost hysteria.

To another Small One concealed in a ventilator at the other end of the corridor, Felix relayed the message exactly as he'd received it. But he had an addition to make. He sent, "Include this. Felix to Whitey. I think I can handle this. Send someone to replace me—I'm on relay duty halfway along corridor Five-C—I'm going to Communications." He wriggled furiously until he made contact with the wall-net, then

launched himself down the corridor towards the intersection leading to the scene of the accident.

Usually Felix left important decisions to the Small
Ones. They had the brains. He didn't know why he'd
taken the initiative this time. Whitey, he thought,
might not be pleased.

He was able to enter the Communications Room
and get to the Small One's body without the crew-man
seeing him. Singer, though impractical in many ways,
could create quite a diversion when he wanted to. Singer was fluttering around the man's head in tight
circles, and the man was making ineffectual grabs at
him and wondering loudly what had got into the
blasted thing. He had eyes and thoughts, Felix knew,
only for Singer. Good.

The fur on the body was badly scorched, and Felix's
nose told him that parts of the underlying flesh were
cooked, too. Suddenly a raw, animal hunger stirred
inside him and began to grow, but he fought it down.
Since the Change had begun, satisfaction of that nature was not for him. Felix batted the tiny corpse
towards the opposite corner of the room, well away
from those all-important circuits, then launched himself after it.

When he'd retrieved it and had it settled between his
paws, he told Singer, "All right, bird-brain. You can
relax. Better leave now—you're supposed to be afraid
of me."

A bright yellow streak of motion, Singer flew out the

door and down the corridor. Before he was out of range he returned, "I *am* afraid of you . . . you . . . *savage!*"

Seconds later the crew-man caught sight of Felix. Pleased, he said, "Felix! Where've you been hiding yourself?" He grabbed Felix by the neck with one hand and pulled himself into a seat with the other. Clipping in and settling Felix on his lap, he went on, "So you caught a mouse, eh, Felix? But what have you been doing with it? Having a barbecue or something?" He stopped talking then, but his mind was busy. He began to stroke the back of Felix's neck.

Felix didn't feel at all like purring, but he knew that it was expected of him. After a while he began to enjoy it in spite of himself, but that didn't stop him from reading the crew-man's thoughts.

A sharp, clear thought—characteristic of the Small Ones—brought him abruptly to full attention. Felix couldn't see the other, but he knew that the Small One was within thirty feet of him—that was the maximum effective range of their telepathy—probably in the emergency spacesuit hanging outside the door that Felix had noticed coming in. The thought said, "Felix, your replacement is in position. Whitey wants you to report."

"Right. Relay this. Felix to Whitey . . ."

For a moment Felix felt awed as he thought of Whitey in Bio-Lab Three—more than half the length of the great Ship away—surrounded by Big Ones, and the Small Ones who weren't on relay duties, and all

of them working on the Escape. And of the other telepathic relays that linked Lab Three with places like
Seed Storage, Central Control, and Engines. . . .
Catching an impatient thought from the Small One
out in the corridor, Felix hastily brought his mind
back to the report.

". . . This Human is not suspicious," he sent. "The
Small One was so badly scorched that the Lab mark-
ings have been obliterated, and he thinks it is a Wild
One from Seed Storage section. He thinks that I have
knocked it against some live wires while playing with
it, and that I'm very lucky I didn't meet the same fate
myself—there's that old 'nine lives' concept again—
but he is wondering why I didn't eat the thing. . . ."

Felix knew that a feeling of shocked revulsion was
left in the wake of his message as it went down the
line. Felix did not share the deep sorrow that the
accident had caused among the more intelligent and
highly-sensitive Small Ones. He took a perverse pleasure
in shocking them sometimes. Without meaning to
they made him feel inferior, envious. Felix wasn't
proud of these feelings, but there wasn't much he
could do about them. The Change was very slow in
him.

". . . He is not interested in checking any of the
room's equipment," Felix continued, "but is impatient
to rejoin the bulk of the crew who are packed into
Astronomy section all trying to get a closer view of
the new planet. He is feeling rebellious at having to
stand watch here at a time like this, and is wondering

sarcastically if the Captain is expecting natives—if any—of the planet below to just ring him up.

"At the back of his mind he is feeling angry because the scoutship is unable to make a landing. But neither he nor anyone else suspect that we were responsible for damaging its Planetary Drive coils. The fact that the replacements are also missing they blame on a clerical error in storing or checking the equipment back home. They don't know we've hidden them."

The Human stopped his stroking of Felix and pushed him gently off his lap. Felix ended, "He intends trying to sleep now. Nobody will be coming here, he knows, and he's a light sleeper anyway." He waited a little anxiously for Whitey's reply.

"You've done well, Felix."

Even though coloured by the personalities of nearly a score of the relay entities, the thought was still warm, congratulatory. Then it changed subtly. "Come to the Lab at once, Felix. There is a transport problem."

"Right," Felix answered. "But before I go; the Human is asleep now. If you send somebody to arrange those disconnected wires so's they'll pass visual inspection, nothing can go wrong here."

He intercepted the reply when he was already halfway to the Lab. He'd been hurrying. It was:

"Thanks, Felix. It is already being done."

When he reached the Lab two of the Big Ones had the ventilator grill moved aside for him. The door was never used for the reason that the Humans kept it fastened, so that opening it would have aroused their suspicions. Felix wriggled through. As he kicked himself across the small anteroom leading into the lab proper he heard the Big Ones sliding the grill back into position. *Nothing*—especially now that they were so near to success—must be allowed to make the crewmen suspect anything wrong. Even the Big Ones, who weren't too bright, understood that.

Felix hadn't been "reaching" with his mind—too much telepathy was still inclined to tire him—so he had no warning of what to expect. Weightless, unable to stop himself, he sailed gracefully into the Lab—right smack into the middle of it.

He was hit five times and sent spinning, his nicely timed dive ruined, by flying Big Ones. And he lost track of how often young Small Ones rammed him. Everybody in the place—*and* their young, too, if any —were in rapid motion, sailing from wall to wall, floor to ceiling, and even corner to corner. It looked like a furry snowstorm. When he succeeded at last in reaching a wall-net, he directed a thought at the white mouse clinging to the fur of a Big One on the other side of the room. The thought was wordless, incoherent, an all-embracing question mark.

"They're practising for the evacuation, Felix," Whitey explained. "And that is the problem I mentioned. Some of them—the young, especially—won't be able to make it." Whitey stopped to give instructions to a Big One who was floundering helplessly out in the middle of the lab. He resumed, "Come over here, Felix. We can 'talk' better at short range."

Felix was again hit several times on the way across

by flying Big Ones. But being in collision with a guinea-pig wasn't painful, merely disconcerting, and he hadn't enough dignity left for that to be hurt. He had just settled beside the Big One bearing Whitey when Singer flew in and joined them. The canary hung, wings folded and turning slowly in the draft from the air-conditioner, just six inches from Felix's nose. Felix wondered suddenly what it would be like to bite his head off.

Radiating shock and panic, Singer flapped desperately out of range. "Stop that, Felix!"

Whitey was really angry at him, with the helpless frustrated anger that is inspired by the constant misbehaviour of a backward child. Ashamed, Felix addressed Singer.

"Sorry, I didn't mean that. I wouldn't hurt you for anything. Come on back."

Singer fluttered back nervously, thinking about horrid, insensitive brutes, and great hairy cannibals. He wasn't completely reassured.

Whitey, his anger gone as quickly as it had come, began to state the problem.

"You two know that we intend to evacuate everyone, and you also know how we're going to leave the Ship —in one of the radio-controlled testing rockets. But we've misjudged badly. The distance from the Lab here to the launching slips is a little over five hundred feet, and now we find that there won't be enough time to get everybody to the rocket.

"You see, several trips will have to be made for the young, and the Big Ones are slow and awkward.

They've never had a chance to practise long-distance weightless travel like us, and they're much worse at it than we'd expected. And they're so slow to learn, some of them. . . ."

So slow to learn, Felix thought sadly. Just like me. He knew that all three of them were thinking about the Change, and how it had affected them personally, as well as the way it affected their species as a whole.

Not one of them knew for sure just why the Change had come about, but there were theories. The generally accepted one was that the prolonged absence of gravity occasioned by the operation of the Ship's overdrive, or the freedom from their home planet's gravitation, or the removal of some hypothetical radiation given off by the home sun, either singly or taken together had caused a change in the cell structure of the small, relatively simple brains of the animals aboard the Ship. Its result was a steady increase in their I.Q.

The Change, however, did not occur at a uniform rate, but varied with the size of the brain concerned. The small-brained mice were affected first. They developed a high intelligence quickly, and with it the faculty for communicating telepathically. And, as well as reading each other's thoughts, they were able to tap the mind of the crew-man who came to the Lab at weekly intervals to replenish the automatic food dispenser which kept them fed.

They learned a lot from him; his duties, his background, what he thought about the other members of the crew, and, most important, the purpose of the Expedition. Also, because he vocalized his thoughts, they learned the language. This increased their understanding of their environment, but it also caused them to make an important assumption based, although they didn't know it, on too little data.

Because the Ship had only been gone from Earth barely four months, and the awful boredom had not yet set in, this particular Human was full to bursting with the glorious thoughts of this first exploration among the stars, the possible colonization of newly discovered planets, and a warm, brotherly feeling towards everybody in general. And he was naturally kind to animals. He was also the only Human whose mind was available to the animals for reading—no other crew-man came within the thirty-foot radius of the Small Ones' telepathy. Their assumption, therefore, was justified.

For six weeks the community of Small Ones existed in the Lab, with servo-mechanisms attending to their every need, happy, contented, and very excited.

They thought they were the Ship's colonists.

Then one day Singer had been put in the Lab. Singer was a completely new species to the Small Ones. He was bright yellow in colour, had "wings" which made it easy for him to move about in the weightless condition of the Ship, and he produced audible vibrations which were very pleasant to hear. Though he wasn't as bright as the Small Ones, the Change had made him telepathic. He had a lot more information to impart about the Ship and its crew, information that left the Small Ones shocked and horrified. He was able to tell them of their true status aboard the Ship, and of the fate that experimental animals could expect when the time came to test the atmosphere, plant-life, and bacteria of a new planet. Singer also told of a ferocious black monster the Humans called "Felix" that roamed the Ship, and how the Humans had put him in here to keep the beast from killing him.

Living was suddenly a grim business. They would try to escape, of course, but the Small Ones knew enough about the operation of the Ship now to realize how small was the opportunity of doing that. And they couldn't leave the Lab even, because of this thing called Felix. If that had been possible they might have been able to create an opportunity for escape, by sabotage or some other means. But the only thing they could do was wait, and hope that the Big Ones, who also lived in the Lab, would be able to take care of "Felix" when they became further advanced.

But the Big Ones had been slow, Felix knew, and their bigness was only relative. Luckily they never had to try taking care of him; a scrap between a guinea-pig—or even several guinea-pigs—and a full-grown cat would have been no contest at all.

Felix had been nosing about outside the Lab one day, hoping to catch himself some food "on the hoof," when he suddenly realized that the animals inside were "talking" to him. The reason for the strange ability he'd noticed in himself in being able to understand the Humans—even when they didn't speak aloud—was explained to him, and very soon he had more important things on his mind than a craving to eat Small Ones. All at once he had become an important person, an *invaluable* person. The way the Small Ones explained it, his wider knowledge of the Ship and its crew, together with his aid in guiding them to certain key spots, would make an escape not only possible, but highly probable. . . .

"Pay attention, Felix!" Whitey radiated sharply. Felix came hastily out of his day-dream, conscious that if he'd been a Human, his face would have been very red.

"I was saying that the Big Ones are slow," Whitey went on, "and awkward. That's partly because we haven't allowed them outside the Lab much; they'd be spotted too easily. But that's the problem now, moving them quickly.

"At the moment I can see no solution. But you two being 'pets,' and having the freedom of the Ship, might be able to suggest something." Whitey paused, and the ghastly wordless images they all knew so well surged up from the back of his mind. Experimentation, vivisection, *murder*. Grimly, he went on, "I don't want to leave anybody behind to *that*—"

He broke off as two reports came, almost simultaneously, from opposite ends of the great Ship.

"Relay from Secondary Engines. Quarter G deceleration has been ordered for three minutes."

"Relay from Control-room. Captain has ordered quarter G deceleration . . ." It was practically a duet.

The telepathic link-ups that ran from all the key points on the Ship to the Lab were fast, efficient, and accurate. But they were just a little slower than the Ship's inter-com system. Some of the animals were able to act on the information before the deceleration hit them, and hang on. The rest dropped, an uneven, struggling layer of grey and brown, onto the forward wall.

Felix landed the way he always did, crouching, and on his feet. Unfortunately he also landed on a group of eight very young Small Ones. The resultant blast of fear and raw, uninhibited anger from their under-developed minds nearly curdled his brains before he was able to reel off. Then he had to counter the bolts of the outraged parent concerned, even though the adult Small One was intelligent enough to realise that none of it was Felix's fault. There were some things that didn't depend on intelligence, Felix real-ised, and mother love was one of them.

Abruptly Felix felt awed at himself. He was the mus-cle man around here—he'd never had thoughts like *that* before. But the feeling left him just as quickly.

While the deceleration lasted Felix listened to the ranting of the Small One, and tried to keep the amuse-ment he felt from showing too much in his mind. He hadn't hurt the youngsters, of course, just frightened them. They were extraordinarily strong for their size, and they were so light that they could take a knocking about that would probably kill Felix. He began to wonder about their toughness, and about the evacuation problem. Suppose . . .

The Small One caught his half-formed thought and radiated a horrified negative. Felix tried to reassure her, but just then weightlessness returned and he launched himself towards Whitey again.

When Felix was still airborne Whitey sent, "I heard some of that, too, Felix. Would you expand on that thought about ferrying the young to the rocket?"

Felix took the mental equivalent of a deep breath. He was acutely conscious of the fact that his thinking, when compared with that of the Small Ones, was slow and almost incoherent at times. But he did his best.

"It is this. I suggest we ferry the young to the launching slips *before* the adults go, instead of at the same time. That way the Big Ones would have only one trip to make, and no matter how inexperienced they were, there would be plenty of time for the journey. With Singer here to help me as look-out, I can transfer them six or eight at a time to the test rocket. And even if the crew-man should see me—"

Whitey interrupted: "*How* are you going to move them, Felix?" Every mind in the room was giving him full attention now.

"By pretending to play with them," Felix answered. Hesitantly, he began to explain. "In the old days, before I knew all about the Change, the crew used to give me things to play with. It was great fun. . . ." He stopped suddenly, feeling ashamed and embarrassed at the confession he'd just made. Hastily, he went on, "That was before I met you, of course.

"But what I want to say is that I know where some of those playthings are. They are soft, spherical, and their fabric is easily opened. The young ones can hide inside them while I push the things along.

"The Humans won't be suspicious of a cat playing with an old rag ball."

Almost before he had completed his thought the objections were coming thick and fast. Felix found it a little frightening; he had never had so many minds thinking at him all at once before like this. But somehow, after the first few minutes, it didn't scare him any more. It was a strange feeling. He still felt awed by their vastly greater intelligence, but not as much as before. Now he respected them—and almost *liked* them—as equals. Possibly it was the nature of the thoughts they were thinking that brought about the change in him. Felix could understand their feelings, but those thoughts hurt.

Impatiently, he interrupted the constant stream of protest. They were beginning to repeat themselves.

"Whitey! Tell them I'm not going to eat the things. . . ."

They didn't believe him.

Oh, the Small Ones knew that he meant what he said, Felix realized, but they didn't trust his—impulses. The less intelligent Big Ones still thought of him as a semi-domesticated carnivore, and wouldn't trust him with their young farther than they could see him. But, he knew if he could convince the Small Ones that his plan would work, they could win over the Big Ones.

Whitey hadn't taken sides in the argument yet, so that left it up to himself. He signalled sharply for attention and felt pleasantly surprised when he got it at once. He began his sales-talk.

"This is the position as I see it at the moment," he sent. "The Ship is in the process of taking up an eight-hour orbit around the first apparently habitable planet to be discovered. The planet, not yet named, is referred to by the crew as Epsilon Aurigae VII, and they are very excited about finding it during the first seven months of their three-year exploratory voyage.

"From our telepathic relay lines to the Ship's control centres we know that this orbiting manoeuvre will be complete in just under three hours, after which most of the crew will be engaged in mapping the planetary surface, studying its weather, or just looking at it through telescopes. Roughly an hour after the Ship takes up its orbit, two of the big testing rockets will be sent down under remote control to the surface, for the purpose of collecting samples of air, soil and liquid from as many widely separate points on the planet as possible. These rockets will be guided automatically, and if everything goes off according to plan, we will be on one of them."

Felix paused. He was thinking about the Small One

who had died so recently in the Communications room.

"We have been able," he went on, "to fix the alarm circuits here on the Ship so that the rocket containing us will apparently behave normally, though actually it will be disabled by us at the first suitable landing point so that we can disembark. But we have only an hour—*less* than an hour, to allow for slip-ups—when the crew will be too busy to notice our movements; and during this period all the animals must be got aboard the test rocket. That means that everyone here, all the Small Ones in Seed Storage, and all the relays scattered about the Ship will have to reach the launching slip and find their places aboard in that short time. And most of them will have to make several trips back and forwards for their young, or—" Felix regarded the untrained and clumsy Big Ones—the people who haven't been able to practise weightless travel.

"Whitey says that this is impossible."

The Small Ones knew all this, Felix thought, and the Big Ones should know it, too. But everybody had developed the habit of explaining things several times to the Big Ones—they weren't very bright yet. . . . Felix got control of himself quickly. That last thought had been tactless. He hoped the Big Ones had been too busy with their own thoughts to notice his slip.

"Now my idea is that we evacuate the young of both species first, and before the orbiting manoeuvre is completed. That way even the clumsiest"—Felix would

have liked to use a kinder word, but it was impossible
to lie with the mind,—"Big Ones will be able to make
their way to the slip in the hour remaining before the
test rocket leaves. Also, with everybody making just
one trip, the risk of discovery by a crew-man will be
practically nil. I think I can handle it, but I'll need a
lot of help."

Felix was trying to give them the idea that he'd be
under their observation all the time, and that even if
he had wanted to, he couldn't pull anything. It was the
only way, he knew, to get them to agree to his plan.

"There will have to be Small Ones at both ends of
the line to load and unload the young, and I'll need
Singer to create a diversion should a crew-man wander
by and want to play with me. And I'll need help with
other things, too. . . ."

Abruptly he wondered why he was taking all this
trouble for them. A short time ago he wouldn't have
bothered. What was happening to him?

He ended simply, "I don't see any other way of doing
it in time."

Later, as he was propelling a lumpy, brightly-
coloured ball filled with eight struggling baby guinea-
pigs along the corridor towards the rocket, Felix
thought how close it had been. When Whitey agreed
to his plan Felix had thought everything would be
settled—after all, he was their leader. But it hadn't
been like that. There had almost been a civil war
before they finally agreed to his plan, and they had

wasted more than half an hour with their arguing. They just didn't trust Felix, it seemed.

At the intersection leading to the launching slip Felix let his load collide with the wall-net, landing partly on top of it to keep the springy mesh from bouncing it back again. His passengers immediately shrieked that they were being murdered and they wanted their mothers. Luckily, Felix thought, it was on the telepathic frequency; had it been audible, men would have come running from all over the Ship. Hastily he reassured the Small One on relay duty in the corridor who was radiating anxiety like a fluorescent light tube. At the other end of the corridor he saw Singer fluttering around in a slow loop. That was the all-clear signal. Felix settled his burden solidly between his fore-paws and chest and kicked himself off again.

He couldn't really blame them for not trusting him, he thought, as the corridor walls drifted slowly past. There was still quite a lot of the savage in him. Much of it was due to the slowness of his Change, but a lot was due also to the crew-men who had brought him aboard as the Ship's mascot. They were the non-specialists on the Ship. They did most of the donkey work, and they were, to put it mildly, decidedly un-couth. From their minds Felix had learned practi-cally everything he knew until the time of his meet-ing up with the Small Ones. The result was that he was inclined to think and act like his erstwhile "mas-ters." The idiom he used when trying to express his thoughts, and his general air of tough cynicism, made it difficult for the others to trust him completely. It was very hard to convince them that his ideas had changed.

Still, even though he wasn't a nice character, the Small Ones were lucky to have him. They were intelligent, Felix knew; the most intelligent and highly-civilized beings on the Ship—and that included the crew. If they'd only had hands, and a more practical approach to solving their problems, they could have taken over the running of the Ship themselves months ago, and got rid of the Humans. But they weren't tough enough, or practical. When there was any time to spare they used their high intelligence to get into philosophical discussions among themselves, and they were, Felix thought pityingly, terribly unrealistic—soft, even. Like Singer in many ways.

Why, when Whitey had begun planning the Escape he'd told Felix—seriously—that nobody was to be hurt, *not even crew members*.

Felix had thought that very funny.

Just before he made contact with the bulkhead at the end of the corridor a sudden surge of acceleration sent him skidding into the wall. Clinging to a section of wall-net he watched his load roll for several yards, then lodge itself none too gently in a corner. The mental uproar from the passengers nearly drowned out the message from a relay somewhere in the vicinity who reported, "Captain has ordered half G acceleration for three seconds."

Now, Felix thought disgustedly, they tell me.

Singer, who was fluttering his wings slowly to compensate for the half G, hovered a few yards away. Anxiously, he asked, "How many more, Felix? There isn't much time left. . . ."

"About a dozen Small Ones, and five of the others," Felix replied as the engines stopped and he began pushing his load through the open air-lock of the Test Rocket blister. "Relax. Two more trips should do it."

But Singer was the worrying type. Supposing Felix was caught at the wrong end of a corridor during a burst of acceleration. A fall of a hundred or more feet, even under quarter weight, would be bad for his passengers. . . .

And it would be bad for him, too, Felix thought grimly. Possibly it would be fatal. He told Singer rather sharply to be quiet. Felix didn't like being reminded of all the unpleasant things that could happen to him.

Both test rockets lay in their slips. Blunt, grey torpedoes, their access panels lay open, and their stiffly-extended antennae made them resemble twenty-foot beetles. Streamlining was unnecessary; the things weren't designed to break speed records, but to cruise about in the atmosphere of the planet being surveyed at a speed that wouldn't damage their sensitive testing gear, and possibly the even more delicate samples they would pick up from time to time. It was this low speed factor that had made the Escape possible. An ordinary missile, or even a message rocket, with an acceleration of fifty or sixty G's would have made a thin stew out of its passengers five seconds after blast-off. He thought the whole thing had depended on luck right from the start. The animals, apart from odd instances like the Communications Room death, seemed to get all the breaks.

Felix didn't like that. He was distrustful of too much good luck.

He gave his load a gentle nudge in the direction of the nearer rocket. It appeared deserted, innocuous, but Felix knew that inside it was a hive of activity. Most of the Small Ones from the nearby Seed Storage section—the "wild" brethren of the Laboratory mice whose job was the provisioning of the rocket—were already in their positions. The rest were hidden at the open access panels waiting to take care of Felix's passengers.

"Here's another bunch of them," Felix thought at the apparently empty hull. He added lightly, "Fragile. Handle with care."

"Right," came the curt response. "We see them."

These particular Small Ones had no sense of humour at all where Felix was concerned, and with good reason. Before the Change had made them too smart to be caught, and before that same Change made Felix a reluctant vegetarian where live meat was concerned, he had hunted them a lot. During the early part of the voyage the carnage in Seed Storage had been shocking. They had never forgotten it, or forgiven him. Felix thought sometimes that living on a planet with the Small Ones wouldn't be much fun with a thing like that between them—he was becoming strangely sensitive about his bloody past—but when he thought of what the human minds were like at times . . .

Angry with himself for some reason, Felix kicked off on the first leg of his return journey to the Lab. He kept telling himself that he didn't care what the Small Ones thought of him. He didn't care at all. But he was an awful liar, he knew.

Transferring the remaining young to the test rocket was a simple, if strenuous job. There was only one point on the route that was dangerous—an intersection visible to anyone who might be standing in the entrance to the Control Room. But there had been too much going on in there for anyone to be hanging about the door, so they hadn't been spotted. Luck was still with them.

Felix waited beside Whitey, with an almost imperceptible weight pressing them against the wall. All around, the animals waited, too; not communicating, but thinking their own personal thoughts. He took what he hoped was his last look around the Lab. One of his cloth balls, he saw, had been stuffed with food from the robot dispenser—even though the Seed Storage people were supposed to handle the food supply end. Somebody was taking no chances. All the cages were open, and both of the ventilator grills above the door had been moved aside. As he watched, the door swung suddenly outwards and hung open under its own weight. The Small One who had been working at the latch jumped free and fell slowly across the room. They were almost ready to go.

If a Human should look in here now, Felix thought, it would be just too bad.

Weight disappeared again as the gentle deceleration ceased. Seconds later a Small One in the tensely-waiting crowd announced, "Relay from Control Room. Captain has ordered kill engines. Orbiting manoeuvre completed."

To everyone in the room Whitey sent, "You know the drill. Nothing can go wrong if we're careful, and if we keep our heads. The relays will give warning if a crew-man intends coming too close to our escape route, minutes before he arrives." Whitey was obviously thinking at the Big Ones as he went on, "There are lots of places to hide along the route if a Human should come—inside the crew's life-suits, for instance —so there is no real danger if you don't panic. Get to the rocket as quickly as possible. And remember, you're on your own.

"The way is clear now. Move off!"

He added, "You first, Felix."

Felix sprang neatly through the Lab door, caught the corridor wall net, and sprang again. An almost-solid mass of dun-coloured animals erupted behind him and began to pile up against the wall facing the door. He caught the sharp, clear thought of Whitey cutting through the growing confusion, trying to sort the mess out and get it moving again. Felix didn't envy him his job.

Felix took up his assigned position—at the inter-section in sight of the Control Room—and waited. There were men in there—he could hear low voices—but the range was too great for him to catch their thoughts. They couldn't have been important anyway, or the relay in there would have passed them on. With a whole new planet to examine, the crew were far too busy to think about the laboratory animals—*yet*.

Eleven Small Ones came sailing along the corridor. They landed against the wall-net almost as one, then launched themselves on the next leg of their journey, still in that tight formation. It was beautiful, Felix thought, but then the Small Ones had had plenty of practice at weightless manoeuvring; besides, one of their greatest sources of pleasure was the execution of the most highly-complicated aerobatics to mind music. They were thinking serious, personal thoughts, but when he asked how the Big Ones were making out, one of them came out of it long enough to send him the mental equivalent of a snort of derision.

When Felix looked back along the corridor he saw what the other had meant.

A kicking, madly-struggling mass of Big Ones had just reached the end of the passage. A few Small Ones were trying to control the resultant pile-up, but without much success. It looked, Felix thought in awe, rather like a cloud of leaves being blown slowly up the corridor by a whirlwind. The Big Ones were moving fast, but they'd no sense of direction at all—they kept bouncing *between* the walls, rapidly, and with a violence that made Felix wince. For every foot they moved forward, they travelled yards sideways, and even at this distance he could hear their panicky squeaking. Some of them definitely weren't keeping their heads. Suddenly worried, Felix sent to the relay near him, "Tell them to stop that noise, or the Humans will *hear* them."

There wasn't much danger of that just yet, of course. His ears were more sensitive than any Human's, but Felix didn't want to take any chances at all.

One of the Big Ones, more by luck than by judgment, came sailing up the middle of the corridor to land on the wall opposite Felix. Pleased, Felix began to radiate grudging approval, then caught what the other was thinking. "Don't," he warned desperately. "Not that way—"

But he was too late. The Big One, disoriented and frightened by his trip, had already taken off from the wall, *and he was headed down the corridor leading to the Control Room!* Felix made some hurried calculations of direction and velocity, hoped fervently they were right, and took off after him.

Even with his stronger muscles giving him greater impetus, they were half-way to the Control Room door before Felix caught up with the other—and then he thought he was going to pass him. But with a series of convulsions that nearly broke his back he got close enough to grab a furry leg in his teeth. He hung on desperately as their different masses and velocities sent them spinning rapidly about their common center of gravity. They smacked hard against the wall, only a few yards from the Control Room. Ignoring the frenzied struggles of the Big One, who was sure his leg was bitten off, Felix transferred his hold to the fur at the back of the other's neck and leapt back the way they'd come. He anchored himself solidly at the intersection.

"*That* way, stupid," he sent angrily, and with a strong jerk of his neck muscles he flung the Big One into the corridor leading to the launching slips.

Abruptly he was sorry. There'd been no time for gentleness, of course, but he'd almost enjoyed mauling the unfortunate Big One back there. The other had been lost, confused, never been outside the Lab before. He shouldn't have. . . . Felix didn't quite know what he shouldn't have done.

"The thought does you credit, Felix."

Whitey had left the brown maelstrom that was boiling past the intersection, and was clinging to the net beside Felix. He had been in the thick of it, trying to keep the Big Ones moving—in the right direction, if possible—and he looked decidedly ruffled. He had been in collision with inanimate walls and over-animated animals alike more times than he could remember, and his nerves were beginning to suffer, too. Felix got all that from his mind in the brief pause before Whitey continued.

"That was fast, accurate thinking back there, Felix," he complimented. "You did very well—you can be proud of it. And when we reach the planet, you're going to do a lot better. . . ."

Suddenly uncomfortable and vaguely frightened at some formless meaning that was behind the other's thought, Felix interrupted hastily.

"Is that the lot?" He indicated a few stragglers floundering after the main group along the corridor leading to the rocket blister.

"Yes, that's all of the Big Ones," Whitey replied. "But the others have been told to wait for a bit. There's enough crowding and confusion as it is, and they, being Small Ones, can move quickly and hide more easily if they're spotted. They'll wait in the Lab until the Big Ones are safely aboard."

But Whitey wasn't to be put off by questions. Returning to his praising of Felix, he said, "You don't have to feel uncomfortable, Felix. Or frightened, either . . . but tell me, what do you think of the Big Ones? And what, in your opinion, makes them think and behave as they do?"

Felix thought that this was a fine time to start a philosophical discussion, but Whitey tactfully ignored that thought, so he began trying to explain how he felt about the slow, unbelievably impractical, but somehow likeable Big Ones. He didn't take long over it as he'd never really thought about them very much.

"You should have thought about them, Felix. You're wrong, completely wrong, in everything you think about them—" Whitey broke off as a straggler came crashing into the wall beside him. He reassured the frightened Big One, told him to take it easy, and sent him on his way again. Then he returned to Felix.

"They're definitely *not* stupid, Felix. Just slow to develop," he explained. "The Change is very gradual in them. With us Small Ones it was different—we Changed and reached our peak very quickly—in a few months, in fact. But now we've found indications that the Big Ones have a much greater potential I.Q. than we have—they are still changing. In a few months' time, Felix, they will be our intellectual equals, *then they will pass us.*" There was no sign of rancour in the thought—Whitey was too highly intelligent and civilized for that—only a great and burning excitement. "Think what this means, Felix. The size of their brains compared with ours . . ."

"*No!*" Felix was frightened, scared. He didn't want to think about it.

"But *yes*, Felix," the other contradicted. He stated solemnly, "You can't avoid the obvious. I am now certain that, barring accidents, you will eventually outstrip all of us. You will be the leader.

"If only," Whitey ended wistfully, "you weren't the only one of you. . . ."

Felix felt suddenly that his brain had turned into a bubbling porridge and was about to squeeze from his ears. Fear and disbelief gradually gave way to belief, and an even greater fear—the fear of *responsibility*. But before he could form a coherent reply, another interruption drove everything else from his mind.

"Observation Room to Whitey," the relay in the corridor reported. "A Human has just left here. Intends walking in direction of launching slips. No fixed purpose—thinks he's in way of specialist crew members." The Small One stopped, waiting instructions.

Three long, agonizing seconds later, he was still waiting.

Felix had never known Whitey to behave like this before. The other's mind was a tight knot of fear and panic. It was an unforeseen and possibly tragic turn of events—just a sheer piece of filthy luck, but, Felix thought with a sudden feeling of pity, Whitey was behaving almost like one of the guinea-pigs.

Suddenly Felix remembered something; he took the initiative.

"Singer! Where's Singer?"

"Here, Felix." Singer was close by, only a few yards around the turn of the corridor.

"You heard that report." It was a statement, not a question. "You've got to intercept that Human, and stop him. Do the same as you did in Communications this morning—but get to him *quickly*. Follow the relay line to Observation, they'll give you his movements.

"And Singer, that is the most important job you ever had. Everything depends on it. You've got to stop that Human from coming here. The Big Ones aren't all aboard the rocket yet, and half the Small Ones are scattered over the Ship on relay duty." He ended grimly, "Stop him, Singer, if you've to peck his eyes out."

"*Felix!*" Singer was shocked again, but he got moving. Felix addressed Whitey:

"Better call in the relays. Singer may not be able to stop that Human, but if he delays him enough to get everyone to the launching compartment . . ."

To the relay beside him Whitey commanded, "Send this. To all Small Ones on relay duty and those waiting in the Lab. Move as quickly as possible to the launching slips—*now*. This supersedes all previous instructions." He paused, then went on to Felix alone, "You really meant that? About blinding the Human?" Horror, and a great sorrow was in the thought. "I cannot allow that, Felix, no matter what happens."

"You can't allow it!" Felix was exasperated. Angry, yet somehow pitying, he went on, "Listen. You tell me I'm going to be boss eventually. Well, I'm taking over *now*—temporarily. You people aren't equipped to fight your way out of this, or anything else. I don't know how you'll be able to exist on the planet if one of its life-forms decides to put up an argument— brains aren't everything, you know. You're just too civilized for your own good. You wouldn't hurt a fly, even if not hurting it was to kill you." Felix became more and more heated as he continued, "With me its different. You need someone like me to protect you. Someone who knows Humans well enough to be able to fight them. I ask you, would you let all our friends be caught and killed in lots of unpleasant ways, just to keep a Human from being messed up a little?

"Before I'd allow *that* to happen, I would kill that Human." He ended viciously, "There are ways an intelligent, trusted cat could do just that."

"Felix, you wouldn't . . . you *can't* take a life—even

a Human life—like that." Horror, revulsion, and a terrible shocked urgency were in the other's thought. "Please don't think like that, Felix. Even injuring him . . ."

In ones and twos, Small Ones were passing them, landing on the wall, and leaping towards the rocket compartment. They were the relays from all over the Ship, making for safety, escape. None of them paid any attention to the argument; they were too busy with their own thoughts.

". . . You wouldn't be able to live with a thing like that on your mind," Whitey went on desperately. "You think you could, now. But later, when you've grown more intelligent, more sensitive . . . You're still a baby, Felix, a young savage, even if—"

One of the Small Ones passing broke in urgently, "Whitey. Singer's in trouble. Couldn't get details, the relay line is breaking up too fast, but it seems the Human got scared and took a swat at him. Broke his wing. Now the Human is taking him to Sick Bay to patch him up."

The Small One hurried on.

Felix used some thought vocalizations that his old "masters" would have envied. Then—

"To all Small Ones who can hear me," he sent as strongly as he could. "If you can get to the rocket within one minute, *move!* If you can't, *take cover!*"

Sick Bay was next door to the launching slips.

The corridor was suddenly empty as the Small Ones

scurried for cover or the launching compartment. Felix knew that less than fifteen minutes remained before the rocket took off. And seconds before that happened, the access panels would close, the inner air-lock would seal itself, and a section of the Ship's hull would swing outwards—all automatically, and pre-timed to a second. If anyone wasn't aboard by that time, it would be just too bad. Felix knew what his own chances of making it were now that this latest crisis had been sprung on them, but he also knew that somebody should take control of the situation at the test rocket. Somebody smart—or in the confusion only a handful would get away. . . .

He had no need to finish the thought. Whitey knew what was required.

"I'll go, Felix. But try to make it yourself. We're going to need you." Whitey tried to be commanding, but there was uneasiness in his thought as he reiterated, "And remember, Felix. I won't allow anyone to be hurt."

"I'll try," Felix replied hastily. "And there'll be no rough stuff unless it's necessary. Get going, Whitey. Luck."

The soft slap of sandals on the wall at the end of the corridor announced the arrival of the Human. The Man didn't notice the rapidly moving Whitey against the light grey paintwork, he came sailing nearer, still unsuspicious. As the other drew level with him, Felix leapt alongside with just enough power in his spring to keep pace with him. He was getting an idea.

The man reacted as expected.

"Uh-uh, Felix," the Human said harshly, "Don't touch," and hastily he transferred the unconscious Singer from his hand to the safety of the inside of his blouse. He was thinking that if Felix tried any tricks with the injured canary he would kick Felix the length of the Ship. The man didn't like cats.

So the crew-man thought he wanted to get at the bird. Good; that was exactly what Felix wanted him to think.

As they drifted nearer the launching compartment, an urgent thought from Whitey told him that there were still a lot of animals milling about outside the rocket. Felix had expected that. He made contact with the wall-net and, just as the Human was approaching the open lock of the launching compartment, he sprang hard at the Human's chest.

He landed with considerable force beside the bulge that was the unfortunate Singer, sunk his claws into the fabric, and began screeching and spitting for all he was worth. Startled and angry, the Human tried to knock him off, all the time thinking of sneaking, treacherous cats trying to eat poor, defenceless birds. When Felix fastened his teeth into the other's sleeve—and into a piece of his arm, too—the Human began to get rough. It was quite a melee.

It ended when a vicious, open-handed smack sent Felix against the wall with a thump that nearly shook his teeth loose. But it had served its purpose; they'd floated past the open air-lock without the Human seeing what was going on inside.

Feeling more dead than alive, Felix watched the crew-man halt himself neatly at the door of Sick Bay. Once in there, Felix knew, even though the launching slips were only yards away, the animals would be safe, because the Human intended to be busy working over Singer for some time. Maybe Felix would be able to make it to the rocket after all. The thought that Singer and some of the Small Ones still in hiding about the Ship would not make it had a dampening effect on his sudden rise in spirits. But, he told himself, he couldn't do anything about that.

The Human had the door open slightly, and was looking backwards over his shoulder to see that Felix wasn't going to sneak in, too, when he stared suddenly along the corridor. His jaw dropped open.

Felix felt the fur rise along his back. There was no need for him to follow the startled crew-man's gaze— he saw what was happening with shocking vividness in the other's mind.

About twenty Small Ones had landed at the intersection at the other end of the corridor. Felix had forgotten about them; they were the ones Whitey had told to stay in the Lab, and because the relays had been called in, they'd had no knowledge of Singer's failure to stop the Human. Watched by the startled crew-man, they took off again as they'd landed—in a tight, geometrically exact formation—in the direction of the launching room's air-lock. They must have seen the Human half-concealed in the door-way as soon as they jumped, but while rushing along the centre of the corridor in weightless flight there was nothing they could do about it.

Of all the blind, senseless, *lousy* luck. If it had happened just one second later the Human would have been safely in Sick Bay. But no. Bitter rage, born of despair, flared suddenly in Felix as he thought how near they'd been to escape—the gentle, impractical, too-intelligent Small Ones, and their slow, apparently stupid, but likeable big brothers. But some of them could be saved yet—the ones already aboard the rocket —if Felix could force himself to act quickly enough.

The initial surprise in the crew-man's mind had given way to an intense curiosity, and there was a slowly gathering suspicion as well. Felix knew he had to act fast. Deliberately he let his rage take root in his mind and grow. He could have controlled it at the start, but instead he fed it with memories, painful and humiliating incidents, anything at all that would fan it to greater heat. For what he knew he had to do Felix would have to be in the proper mood. He no longer trusted himself—or the soft, sentimental way he'd begun to think lately.

From inside the launching compartment Whitey's thought beat at him, desperately urging him to stop, to *think*. But it was like a cup of water on a forest fire. His rage mounted. Hazily he knew that the crowd of Small Ones had landed at the air-lock and that Whitey was giving them orders, but the thoughts didn't register. His rage grew to a blazing, white-hot fury, and his eyes never left the crew-man.

The Human hung about ten yards away, with one hand holding the door and the other inside his blouse, defenceless. Vaguely, Felix knew that all the Small Ones were thinking at him now, but it had no effect at all.

For an instant he tensed for the spring, calculating, watching the Human's face. Then, with black murder in his heart, he leapt at the other's eyes.

He never reached them.

The mass and inertia of a moving Small One is inconsiderable, but twenty of them, leaping together and hitting him as one, was more than enough to deflect his dive towards the Human. Felix crashed into the wall-net amid a cloud of Small Ones, two feet away from the crew-man. He was too shocked by the turn of events to move, but the Human wasn't. Kicking himself free of the doorway he drifted up the corridor, thinking that if he didn't get out of here quick he'd be drowned in living mice; and then thinking that mice shouldn't behave like that, and that Felix shouldn't . . .

Suddenly the Human's thoughts began to jump around. Instances, apparently unrelated, were linking up in his mind. Wires gnawed through, small components missing, tiny but important gadgets sabotaged. Could it be . . . Just then his jump carried him past the open lock of the launching compartment. He saw what was happening inside.

Felix hadn't realised how quiet it had been until the General Alarm siren blared out. Senses dulled with despair, he watched the crew-man jabbering into a wall 'phone and holding the Alarm button down with a hard-pressed palm. Voices began approaching from all over the Ship; excited, slightly frightened voices. Thoughts followed them as the crew-man at the inter-com broadcast his suspicions—the wary, coldly-im-placable thoughts born in the brains of the most fero-cious and deadly beast of all, *man*.

But, Felix knew, these beasts were logical. They would realize that they still needed experimental ani-mals for the planets they hoped to find. They would not, he hoped fervently, slaughter all his friends right away.

But if they were too angry, they wouldn't behave logically.

Through the direct observation port Captain Erics-son watched a star that blazed like a gorgeous sapphire against a background of scattered silver dust. Home. He could almost see it coming closer. Smiling, he stroked the cat that sat on his shoulder, serenely following his gaze.

"Good thing your friends didn't make it to that first planet, Felix," he said reminiscently. "That virus . . . They wouldn't have lasted a week. But they should do all right on the world we picked for them. No ani-mal life to speak of, but a semi-intelligent plant-life to keep them from getting too lazy. Unless . . ."

Unless the gravity of their new planet brought about a reversal in the Change that had taken place in space, he was thinking. Even he didn't know for certain whether it was the prolonged absence of weight that had caused it, or some enigmatic radiation given off by their home sun, Sol. That was why Felix had elected to remain on the Ship. A cat among a colony of mice and guinea-pigs, and all of them degenerating . . . It wasn't a pretty thought.

As he addressed the others in the room, the tremendous being that Captain Ericsson had become used spoken words. They would be orbiting Earth in three days, and he wanted to become accustomed to communicating non-telepathically again. He said, "We are not going to like the Earth, even though it is our home. We've . . . outgrown it. The Change in us humans, with our larger and more complex brain structure, was very slow indeed—it took almost two years before our maximum development was attained. But even Felix here, who looks on us as near deities, is incapable of realizing just how much we have matured." He paused, shaking his head gravely. "No. It is our duty to report the habitable planets we've found, the Change that takes place in space, everything. And they will want some of us for psychological testing. But we will not like Earth. On Earth they fight, and hate, and do violence. They . . . they *kill.*

"I think we will want to leave again as quickly as we can."

Journeys End

BY POUL ANDERSON

Poul Anderson's stories usually are distinguished by an underlying tone of basic optimism, a feeling that mankind can deal with almost any kind of situation, given enough perseverance and ingenuity. This short and shocking story is an exception, though: dark, bitter, heartbreaking, a nightmarish exploration of the notion that full communication between minds can lead to the deepest kind of love.

—*doctor bill & twinges in chest but must be all right maybe indigestion & dinner last night & wasn't audrey giving me the glad eye & how the hell is a guy to know & maybe i can try and find out & what a fool I can look if she doesn't—*

—*goddam idiot & they shouldn't let some people*

256

*drive & oh all right so the examiner was pretty lenient
with me i haven't had a bad accident yet & christ
blood all over my blood let's face it i'm scared to drive
but the buses are no damn good & straight up three
paces & man in a green hat & judas i ran that red
light—*

In fifteen years a man got used to it, more or less.
He could walk down the street and hold his own
thoughts to himself while the surf of unvoiced voices
was a nearly ignored mumble in his brain. Now and
then, of course, you got something very bad, it stood
up in your skull and shrieked at you.

Norman Kane, who had come here because he was
in love with a girl he had never seen, got to the corner
of University and Shattuck just when the light turned
against him. He paused, fetching out a cigaret with
nicotine-yellowed fingers while traffic slithered in front
of his eyes.

It was an unfavorable time, four-thirty in the afternoon, homeward rush of nervous systems jangled with
weariness and hating everything else on feet or wheels.
Maybe he should have stayed in the bar down on San
Pablo. It had been pleasantly cool and dim, the bar-
tender's mind an amiable cud-chewing somnolence,
and he could have suppressed awareness of the
woman.

No, maybe not. When the city had scraped your
nerves raw, they didn't have much resistance to the
slime in some heads.

Odd, he reflected, how often the outwardly polite
ones were the foully twisted inside. They wouldn't

dream of misbehaving in public, but just below the surface of consciousness . . . Better not think of it, better not remember. Berkeley was at least preferable to San Francisco or Oakland. The bigger the town, the more evil it seemed to hold, three centimeters under the frontal bone. New York was almost literally uninhabitable.

There was a young fellow waiting beside Kane. A girl came down the sidewalk, pretty, long yellow hair and a well-filled blouse. Kane focused idly on her: yes, she had an apartment of her own, which she had carefully picked for a tolerant superintendent. Lechery jumped in the young man's nerves. His eyes followed the girl, Cobean-style, and she walked on . . . simple harmonic motion.

Too bad. They could have enjoyed each other. Kane chuckled to himself. He had nothing against honest lust, anyhow not in his liberated conscious mind; he couldn't do much about a degree of subconscious puritanism. Lord, you can't be a telepath and remain any kind of prude. People's lives were their own business, if they didn't hurt anyone else too badly.

—*the trouble is,* he thought, *they hurt me. but i can't tell them that. they'd rip me apart and dance on the pieces. the government /the military/ wouldn't like a man to be alive who could read secrets but their fear-inspired anger would be like a baby's tantrum beside the red blind amok of the common man (thoughtful husband considerate father good honest worker earnest patriot) whose inward sins were known. you can talk to a priest or a psychiatrist be-*

cause it is only talk & and he does not live your fail-
ings with you—

The light changed and Kane started across. It was clear fall weather, not that this area had marked seasons, a cool sunny day with a small wind blowing up the street from the water. A few blocks ahead of him, the University campus was a splash of manicured green under brown hills.

—flayed & burningburningburning moldering rotted flesh & the bones the white hard clean bones coming out gwtjklfmx—

Kane stopped dead. Through the vertigo he felt how sweat was drenching into his shirt.

And it was such an ordinary-looking man!

"Hey, there, buster, wake up! Ya wanna get killed?"

Kane took a sharp hold on himself and finished the walk across the street. There was a bench at the bus stop and he sat down till the trembling was over.

Some thoughts were unendurable.

He had a trick of recovery. He went back to Father Schliemann. The priest's mind had been like a well, a deep well under sun-speckled trees, its surface brightened with a few gold-colored autumn leaves . . . but there was nothing bland about the water, it had a sharp mineral tang, a smell of the living earth. He had often fled to Father Schliemann, in those days of puberty when the telepathic power had first wakened in him. He had found good minds since then, happy minds, but never one so serene, none with so much strength under the gentleness.

"I don't want you hanging around that papist, boy,

do you understand?" It was his father, the lean implac- able man who always wore a black tie. "Next thing you know, you'll be worshiping graven images just like him."

"But they *aren't*—"

His ears could still ring with the cuff. "Go up to your room! I don't want to see you till tomorrow morning. And you'll have two more chapters of Deuteronomy memorized by then. Maybe that'll teach you the true Christian faith."

Kane grinned wryly and lit another cigaret from the end of the previous one. He knew he smoked too much. And drank—but not heavily. Drunk, he was defense- less before the horrible tides of thinking.

He had had to run away from home at the age of fourteen. The only other possibility was conflict end- ing with reform school. It had meant running away from Father Schliemann too, but how in hell's red fire could a sensitive adolescent dwell in the same house as his father's brain? Were the psychologists now admitting the possibility of a sadistic masochist? Kane *knew* the type existed.

Give thanks for this much mercy, that the extreme telepathic range was only a few hundred yards. And a mind-reading boy was not altogether helpless; he could evade officialdom and the worst horrors of the under- world. He could find a decent elderly couple at the far end of the continent and talk himself into adoption.

Kane shook himself and got up again. He threw the cigaret to the ground and stubbed it out with his heel. A thousand examples told him what obscure sexual symbolism was involved in the act, but what the deuce . . . it was also a practical thing. Guns are phallic too, but at times you need a gun.

Weapons: he could not help wincing as he recalled dodging the draft in 1949. He'd traveled enough to know this country was worth defending. But it hadn't been any trick at all to hoodwink a psychiatrist and get himself marked hopelessly psychoneurotic—which he would be after two years penned with frustrated men. There had been no choice, but he could not escape a sense of dishonor.

—*haven't we all sinned / every one of us / is there a single human creature on earth without his burden of shame?*—

A man was coming out of the drugstore beside him. Idly, Kane probed his mind. You could go quite deeply into anyone's self if you cared to, in fact you couldn't help doing so. It was impossible merely to scan verbalized thinking: the organism is too closely integrated. Memory is not a passive filing cabinet, but a continuous process beneath the level of consciousness; in a way, you are always reliving your entire past. And the more emotionally charged the recollection is, the more powerfully it radiates.

The stranger's name was—no matter. His personality was as much an unchangeable signature as his fingerprints. Kane had gotten into the habit of thinking of people as such-and-such a multidimensional symbolic topography; the name was an arbitrary gabble.

The man was an assistant professor of English at

the University. Age forty-two, married, three children, making payments on a house in Albany. Steady sober type, but convivial, popular with his colleagues, ready to help out most friends. He was thinking about tomorrow's lectures, with overtones of a movie he wanted to see and an undercurrent of fear that he might have cancer after all, in spite of what the doctor said.

Below, the list of his hidden crimes. As a boy: tormenting a cat, well-buried Oedipean hungers, masturbation, petty theft . . . the usual. Later: cheating on a few exams, that ludicrous fumbling attempt with a girl which came to nothing because he was too nervous, the time he crashed a cafeteria line and had been shoved away with a cold remark (and praises be, Jim who had seen that was now living in Chicago) . . . still later: wincing memories of a stomach uncontrollably rumbling at a formal dinner, that woman in his hotel room the night he got drunk at the convention, standing by and letting old Carver be fired because he didn't have the courage to protest to the dean . . . now: youngest child a nasty whining little snotnose, but you can't show anyone what you really think, reading Rosamond Marshall when alone in his office, disturbing young breasts in tight sweaters, the petty spite of academic politics, giving Simonson an undeserved good grade because the boy was so beautiful, disgraceful sweating panic when at night he considered how death would annihilate his ego—

And what of it? This assistant professor was a good

man, a kindly and honest man, his inwardness ought
to be between him and the Recording Angel. Few of
his thoughts had ever become deeds, or ever would.
Let him bury them himself, let him be alone with
them. Kane ceased focusing on him.

The telepath had grown tolerant. He expected little
of anyone; nobody matched the mask, except possibly
Father Schliemann and a few others . . . and those
were human too, with human failings; the difference
was that they knew peace. It was the emotional overtones of guilt which made Kane wince. God knew he
himself was no better. Worse, maybe, but then his life
had thrust him to it. If you had an ordinary human
sex drive, for instance, but could not endure to co-
habit with the thoughts of a woman, your life became
one of fleeting encounters; there was no help for it,
even if your austere boyhood training still protested.

"Pardon me, got a match?"

*—lynn is dead / i still can't understand it that i will
never see her again & eventually you learn how to go
on in a chopped-off fashion but what do you do in the
meantime how do you get through the nights alone—*

"Sure."—*maybe that is the worst: sharing sorrow
and unable to help & only able to give him a light for
his cigaret—*

Kane put the matches back in his pocket and went
on up University, pausing again at Oxford. A pair of
large campus buildings jutted up to the left; others
were visible ahead and to the right, through a screen
of eucalyptus trees. Sunlight and shadow damascened

the grass. From a passing student's mind he discovered where the library was. A good big library—perhaps it held a clue, buried somewhere in the periodical files. He had already arranged for permission to use the facilities: prominent young author doing research for his next novel.

Crossing wistfully named Oxford Street, Kane smiled to himself. Writing was really the only possible occupation: he could live in the country and be remote from the jammed urgency of his fellow men. And with such an understanding of the soul as was his, with any five minutes on a corner giving him a dozen stories, he made good money at it. The only drawback was the trouble of avoiding publicity, editorial summonses to New York, autographing parties, literary teas . . . he didn't like those. But you could remain faceless if you insisted.

They said nobody but his agent knew who B. Traven was. It had occurred, wildly, to Kane that Traven might be another like himself. He had gone on a long journey to find out. . . . No. He was alone on earth, a singular and solitary mutant, except for—

It shivered in him, again he sat on the train. It had been three years ago, he was in the club car having a nightcap while the streamliner ran eastward through the Wyoming darkness. They passed a westbound train, not so elegant a one. His drink leaped from his hand to the floor and he sat for a moment in stinging blindness. That flicker of thought, brushing his mind and coming aflame with recognition and then borne away again . . . Damn it, damn it, he should have pulled the emergency cord and so should *she*. They should have halted both trains and stumbled through cinders and sagebrush and found each other's arms.

Too late. Three years yielded only a further emptiness. Somewhere in the land there was, or there had been, a young woman, and she was a telepath and the startled touch of her mind had been gentle. There had not been time to learn anything else. Since then he had given up on private detectives. (How could you tell them: "I'm looking for a girl who was on such-and-such a train the night of—"?) Personal ads in all the major papers had brought him nothing but a few crank letters. Probably she didn't read the personals; he'd never done so till his search began, there was too much unhappiness to be found in them if you understood humankind as well as he did.

Maybe this library here, some unnoticed item . . . but if there are two points in a finite space and one moves about so as to pass through every infinitesimal volume dV, it will encounter the other one in finite time *provided* that the other point is not moving too.

Kane shrugged and went along the curving way to the gatehouse. It was slightly uphill. There was a bored cop in the shelter, to make sure that only authorized cars were parked on campus. The progress paradox: a ton or so of steel, burning irreplaceable petroleum to shift one or two human bodies around, and doing the job so well that it becomes universal and chokes the cities which spawned it. A telepathic society would be more rational. When every little wound in the child's soul could be felt and healed . . . when the thick burden of guilt was laid down, because everyone knew that everyone else had done the same . . . when men could not kill, because soldier and murderer felt the victim die . . .

—adam & eve? you can't breed a healthy race out of two people. but if we had telepathic children/ & we would be bound to do so i think because the mutation is obviously recessive/ then we could study the heredity of it & the gift would be passed on to other bloodlines in logical distribution & every generation there would be more of our kind until we could come out openly & even the mindmutes could be helped by our psychiatrists & priests & each would be fair and clean and sane—

There were students sitting on the grass, walking under the Portland Cement Romanesque of the buildings, calling and laughing and talking. The day was near an end. Now there would be dinner, a date, a show, maybe some beer at Robbie's or a drive up into the hills to neck and watch the lights below like trapped stars and the mighty constellation of the Bay Bridge . . . or perhaps, with a face-saving grumble about mid-terms, an evening of books, a world suddenly opened. It must be good to be young and mindmute. A dog trotted down the walk and Kane relaxed into the simple wordless pleasure of being a healthy and admired collie.

—so perhaps it is better to be a dog than a man?

no/ surely not/ for if a man knows more grief he also knows more joy & so it is to be a telepath: more easily hurt yes but /god/ think of the mindmutes always locked away in aloneness and think of sharing not only a kiss but a soul with your beloved—

The uphill trend grew steeper as he approached the library, but Kane was in fair shape and rather enjoyed the extra effort. At the foot of the stairs he paused for a quick cigaret before entering. A passing woman flicked eyes across him and he learned that he could also smoke in the lobby. Mind reading had its everyday uses. But it was good to stand here in the sunlight. He stretched, reaching out physically and mentally.

—let's see now the integral of log x dx well make a substitution suppose we call y equal to log x then this is interesting i wonder who wrote that line about euclid has looked on beauty bare—

Kane's cigaret fell from his mouth.

It seemed that the wild hammering of his heart must drown out the double thought that rivered in his brain, the thought of a physics student, a very ordinary young man save that he was quite wrapped up in the primitive satisfaction of hounding down a problem, and the other thought, the one that was listening in.

—she—

He stood with closed eyes, asway on his feet, breathing as if he ran up a mountain. *—are You there? are You there?—*

—not daring to believe: what do i feel?—

—*i was the man on the train*—

—*& i was the woman*—

A shuddering togetherness.

"Hey! Hey, mister, is anything wrong?"

Almost Kane snarled. Her thought was so remote, on the very rim of indetectability, he could get nothing but subvocalized words, nothing of the self, and this busybody—"No, thanks, I'm OK, just a, a little winded."—*where are You, where can i find You o my darling?*—

—*image of a large white building/right over here & they call it dwinelle hall & i am sitting on the bench outside & please come quickly please be here i never thought this could become real*—

Kane broke into a run. For the first time in fifteen years, he was unaware of his human surroundings. There were startled looks, he didn't see them, he was running to her and she was running too.

—*my name is norman kane & i was not born to that name but took it from people who adopted me because i fled my father (horrible how mother died in darkness & he would not let her have drugs though it was cancer & he said drugs were sinful and pain was good for the soul & he really honestly believed that & when the power first appeared i made slips and he beat me and said it was witchcraft & i have searched all my life since & i am a writer but only because i must live but it was not aliveness until this moment*—

—*o my poor kicked beloved/ i had it better/ in me*

*the power grew more slowly and i learned to cover it
& i am twenty years old & came here to study but
what are books at this moment—*

He could see her now. She was not conventionally
beautiful, but neither was she ugly, and there was
kindness in her eyes and on her mouth.

*—what shall i call you? to me you will always be
You but there must be a name for the mindmutes &
i have a place in the country among old trees & such
few people as live nearby are good folk/ as good as life
will allow them to be—*

*—then let me come there with you & never leave
again—*

They reached each other and stood a foot apart.
There was no need for a kiss or even a handclasp . . .
not yet. It was the minds which leaped out and enfolded and became one.

—I REMEMBER THAT AT THE AGE OF THREE I DRANK
OUT OF THE TOILET BOWL/ THERE WAS A PECULIAR
FASCINATION TO IT & I USED TO STEAL LOOSE CHANGE
FROM MY MOTHER THOUGH SHE HAD LITTLE ENOUGH
TO CALL HER OWN SO I COULD SNEAK DOWN TO THE
DRUGSTORE FOR ICE CREAM & I SQUIRMED OUT OF THE
DRAFT & THESE ARE THE DIRTY EPISODES INVOLVING
WOMEN—

—AS A CHILD I WAS NOT FOND OF MY GRANDMOTHER
THOUGH SHE LOVED ME AND ONCE I PLAYED THE FOL-
LOWING FIENDISH TRICK ON HER & AT THE AGE OF
SIXTEEN I MADE AN UTTER FOOL OF MYSELF IN THE
FOLLOWING MANNER & I HAVE BEEN PHYSICALLY

CHASTE CHIEFLY BECAUSE OF FEAR BUT MY VICARIOUS
EXPERIENCES ARE NUMBERED IN THE THOUSANDS—
    Eyes watched eyes with horror.
    *—it is not that you have sinned for i know everyone
has done the same or similar things or would if they
had our gift & i know too that it is nothing serious or
abnormal & of course you have decent instincts &
are ashamed—*
    *—just so/ it is that you know what i have done &
you know every last little wish & thought & buried
uncleanness & in the top of my head i know it doesn't
mean anything but down underneath is all which was
drilled into me when i was just a baby & i will not admit to* ANYONE *else that such things exist in* ME—
    A car whispered by, homeward bound. The trees
talked in the light sunny wind.
    A boy and girl went hand in hand.
    The thought hung cold under the sky, a single
thought in two minds.
    —get out i hate your bloody guts.—